MATED MINOTAUR

MATED MYTHS

"WHAT IS A LITTLE DRY HUMPING BETWEEN FRIENDS?"

LEX LOGAN

Cover design and formatting by Alisha Conolly

Cover illustration by Azukiarts

Editing by Laura Ibic at Hummingbird Editing

CONTENTS

Author Note

The Mate Myths series is inspired by ancient Greek mythology. I have taken creative liberties in the descriptions and abilities of characters, places, and objects.

Please do not go into this with expectations of historical accuracy, it is fiction after all.

Mated Minotaur is book three of a six-book series of interconnected standalones.

While each book can be read separately and will have their own HEA/HFN, you will have the best reading experience if read in order.

Please be advised that some matter in this book may be triggering for some readers.

The next page covers the content warnings for Mated Minotaur.

Content Warnings

Mated Minotaur contains but is not limited to: graphic violence, explicit sexual content and scenes, kidnapping, drugging, domestic violence (historical), non-human sexual appendages, law enforcement misconduct.

Kinks including but not limited to: primal play, knotting, breeding (no pregnancy)

If you believe something has been missed, please reach out to lexloganauthor@gmail.com

This one is for me.

1

Katie

There are certain points in our lives that have us sit back and re-evaluate the choices that lead us to each pivotal moment. Sometimes they seem inevitable, and no matter which way you look at it or imagine the different scenarios, the result turns out the same. For most people, that decision usually isn't centered around shooting their abusive ex, going on the run, and facing down one of his goons who has you cornered in the public library. But here I am.

I thought I would find respite within the warm and inviting library walls, but instead, I find myself on the run. Again. How Greg's goon tracked me down, I have no idea, but I'm not about to hang around and find out.

He utters a string of curses as the librarian pushes her returns trolley into him, and I use the distraction to hightail it out of there. I just wish I could've seen the look on his face. Thank sweet baby

Jesus for the librarian who recognized a girl in need. She might be my hero.

I don't waste a second, ducking out through the worn timber doors and heading into the park attached to the library, hoping the trees will obscure me long enough to get to the other side. I pull the hood of my jacket lower over my eyes as the afternoon chill of fall sends a shiver down my spine, falling into a jog when I catch sight of a bus pulling up at the closest stop. Breathless, I manage to jump aboard at the last moment, the doors snapping closed behind me. I didn't have time to check where it was headed; as long as it's anywhere but here, that's fine with me. Tension rides me as I find a seat near the back and watch the high rises of the city slide past in a blur. I only let myself relax when I eventually make it to the outskirts of the city without noticing anybody following me. I jump off the bus, stuffing my hands into my pockets to keep them warm. The gray concrete landscape is depressing, and the lack of people around does nothing to ease my paranoia. I check over my shoulder before heading into the restroom attached to the exterior of a gas station. Ignoring the shit-stained toilet, I splash my face with cold water. I squeeze my shaky hands into fists, willing them to stop, before slapping the edge of the porcelain basin. *That was really fucking close.*

A sinking pit of dread opens in my stomach when I exit the filthy gas station bathroom to find that very same man waiting for me, leaning against the brick wall outside the door with a lit cigarette hanging from his mouth.

"You cannot outrun Fate, girly." He takes a drag, blowing a smoke ring in my face.

I stifle a cough, my eyes darting around the parking lot, quickly assessing my surroundings and if anyone might come to the assistance of a girl being harassed by a menacing-looking man, and find it deserted. Typical. Any hope I have of a good samaritan coming to save the day deflates like a popped balloon. It's a good thing I've learned a lot about how to save myself since I shot Greg. Going on the run and living on the streets will do that for a girl. Without hesitation, I run—

Straight into the arms of another man who rounds the corner of the building, his arms already outstretched and waiting to catch me, like he knew exactly where I was going to be at that moment. I struggle and screech as strong arms band around my body, trapping my own at my sides. I kick and buck and scream, making as much noise as possible, hoping to draw any attention. Throwing my head back, I smack the man in the face with the back of my skull. Pain bands around my head, but it's enough for him to let me go, cradling his bloody nose.

"Lachesis! She—she headbutted me!" The wounded man stomps his foot on the cement. If I wasn't scared for my life, I would find it comical.

The first man—Lachesis—sighs, dropping his cigarette and stomping it out beneath his boot before entering the metaphorical ring. I back up, keeping both of them in my sight as they cage me against the building. With not many options available to me, I reach for my last resort. Sliding my hand into my pocket, I pull out a small red pocketknife, flicking the blade open and wielding it in front of myself.

"Stay back!" I wave my arm wildly, leaping forward and back to swipe at the injured one, who screeches, bringing his arms up to shield his face. It leaves me with a small opening, and I take it, bolting for the street.

Lachesis curses, and pounding footsteps on the pavement let me know he's on my tail. I can't help but throw a quick glance over my shoulder.

"Why do they always run?" the injured one whines, following up the rear.

Panting, I turn my eyes back to the path. There's no way I'm going to be able to outrun them. Their longer stride eats the distance between us in half the time it takes me to create it. I won't go down without a fight, though. I got free from Greg, and I'm never going back.

A beat-up-looking camper van turns into the street. Hope blooms at the thought that someone might help me. I run in its direction, waving my arms above my head.

"Help! Please stop!"

Sheer relief fills me when it slows to a stop, idling by the curb as I run up to the passenger side door, shoving my knife back in my pocket. The driver leans over to wind the window down.

"Please, you have to help me!" I say between pants. "These men are chasing me."

The elderly woman behind the wheel looks past me, seeing the two men running down the sidewalk toward us. Her brow furrows, and she nods to herself.

"Get in, girly." Her voice is no more than a rasp, as if she's smoked a pack of cigarettes a day for her entire life. I don't hesitate, swinging the door open and jumping in, slamming the lock down behind me, right as the two men reach us.

The camper van is old. A vintage orange curtain separates the front cabin from the back, and I have to manually wind the window up as they bang against the door and try to reach inside.

I scream, swatting at their hands as I try to get the window closed, jamming the injured one's fingers at the top when he doesn't pull them out fast enough. He howls, yanking them free, and I finish the job, blocking out the noise as the window finally shuts.

I fall back into my seat with a sigh, my chest pounding from the adrenaline coursing through my veins.

"Thanks." I brush my bangs off my sweaty forehead, giving the old lady a shaky smile.

"It is lucky Fate had me show up when I did, girly," she croaks with a toothless smile.

My blood runs cold. What an odd choice of words. I recall what Lachesis said about how I couldn't outrun Fate. He called me girly, too.

"Um, you know what, I think I've made a mistake." My voice shakes.

"It is too late, Katie." She tips her head back and cackles.

How does she know my name? I go to unlock the door, unease crawling up my neck. I'd rather take my chances out there than here. I reach for the handle and realize it's missing from the inside of the door. Panic spikes, my head whipping around for anything that might help me get out of here. I hear the rear passenger door slide open on a click. Tears well in my eyes as my throat chokes up in fear.

"Please, no," I whisper. *Please don't take me back to Greg*, I silently pray.

The orange curtain parts behind me, and cold, skeletal hands wrap around my face, pressing a sweet-smelling cloth to my nose, muffling my screams.

2

KATIE

The first thing I feel is the splitting pain in my skull, as if someone has taken an axe to it, cracking me open and spilling its contents like a bowl of jelly knocked onto the floor. My stomach roils, the nausea convincing me to keep my eyes closed because I know if I open them, the world will be spinning. I stave off the inherent need to roll over and empty my guts, breathing in deeply through my nose and out through my mouth. My ears are filled with a tinny ring, and I know from experience that I have a concussion. My clothes cling to my skin as if someone has dunked me in the water. A pitiful groan escapes me, tears rimming my eyes.

I scrunch my hands into fists at my side, sand sifting through my fingers. *Wait.* I pause, opening my hands and patting the ground beneath me. Sand sticks to them. My carefully thought-out breathing hitches. I've seen a beach only once before. It was a full day's drive from home to the coast on a day that Greg was being particularly forgiving, right after he had given me a black eye. Back then, I thought it was because he felt guilty for the outburst, but I know better now. I really should have aimed for something more vital when I shot him. The kneecap was much too lenient a punishment.

I hesitate to open my eyes, namely because my skull is screaming at me, and because I feel the granules around me shift slightly as heavy footsteps reverberate through the sand. My instincts tell me to play dead. The guttural noise of an animal sounds somewhere close by—grunts and snuffles. There's a returning grunt, and I realize there's more than one. My heart hammers behind my chest, my nausea pushed to the side.

My thoughts race, running through a list of animals I might encounter in the wild. If we're near the coast, it could be lizards of some kind. That wouldn't be too bad. I could probably outrun a lizard. Maybe. How fast can lizards run? It could be a bear. Do we have bears here? Fear has my thoughts spiraling out of control. I cock an eyelid, just barely a sliver, my lashes blurring most of my vision. Something stands above me, the bright blue cloudless sky bathing it in shadows. My heartbeat stutters.

Red scales come into view as it leans down close, its head cocked to the side, and sniffs. I lay rooted to the spot, frozen in fear and holding my breath. Large membraned wings flex behind it, and a tail flicks in what I can only describe as agitation as it grunts to its… friend? Lizard thing? *What the fuck.* Another deep sniff and a growl before it turns its attention elsewhere, stepping over me with clawed feet. I don't dare move to peek at what they're doing. They continue to grunt at each other in some sort of language, their voices growing distant until I can no longer hear them. Not a bear.

My brain screams at me to take a breath, unable to hold it any longer. I can either die from suffocation or die at the hands of whatever the fuck that was. I suck in a ragged gasp of air, my eyes flinging themselves wide open before flinching against the harsh sun. I roll onto my stomach, pushing myself up onto my hands and knees, and vomit. Stomach acid burns my throat and nose on its way up, splattering on the sand. I gasp. *What the fuck was that?*

It—*they*—looked like aliens, from what I could see, and I swear to God, if I've been abducted by aliens, I'll be—well, actually, will I be mad? I mean, yes, I'll be mad if they want to eat me. But they didn't seem interested, so I'm not a food source. Yet. Being abducted by aliens wouldn't be the worst thing that's ever happened to me, and it could be an improvement on my current situation, if I remain not-food. But I'm not going to wait for them to change their minds.

I stagger to my feet, my stomach still upset, and clench my teeth against the ache of a concussion. I need to find somewhere safe, then assess myself for injuries. Unfortunately, this is a routine I already know all too well. I kick up the sand beneath me in my haste to get off this cursed beach and the monsters that might be lurking between the sand dunes.

My soggy jeans and jacket do nothing to cool me down beneath the beating sun as they quickly dry, the saltwater causing them to stiffen around my limbs. My head pounds, and my pulse thumps in my ears as if my brain has been battered against the inside of my skull. Heart hammering, I slip. My hands hit the hot sand before I catch a mouthful of it. I scrabble to my feet, throwing a quick look over my shoulder, checking to make sure I'm not being followed. Two halves of a ruined shipping container lay half-submerged in the water. I can only assume that's how I got here. I shudder at the thought of being trapped inside it. How I ended up in one is a total mystery to me. Everything is fuzzy. The last thing I can remember is the library, one of Greg's goons finding me, and the evil old woman who locked me in her camper van. My stomach turns.

If I wasn't abducted by aliens, what were those things? Shaking my head, I pick myself up and push on. Soon enough, the sand dunes tuck the wreckage away, and I can convince myself the lizard monsters were never there, and neither was I.

The dunes and sand eventually give way to pebbles and rocks the further inland I get. Scraggly tufts of grass poke through in bits and pieces, and everything crunches beneath my boots. The smell of saltwater carries inwards on the light breeze, but it's not enough to stifle the heat. My bangs are plastered to my forehead. I'm drenched in sweat from the tip of my nose, running down my spine, and beading behind my knees. It's an uncomfortable feeling, but nothing compared to the idea of being something's next meal. I think about ditching my jacket, but the baby tee beneath leaves my pale flesh too exposed to the sun's harsh rays. For all I know, we could be on the East Coast, or we could be somewhere in the middle of the ocean.

The sea breeze and heat, however, are a far cry from the cool fall chill from home, and I fear the latter is most likely.

Further inland, craggy hills break up the landscape, and a jagged mountain reaches high into the clouds. There's no sign of human civilization between me and the mountain, and the truth of my situation sinks heavy in my gut. Alone, in the wild, with no one to know where to begin to look for me. Too bad the only person that might bother is the one person I don't want to find me.

Living on the streets and being on the run from Greg's goons has taught me a few good lessons. One is that I'm used to a lot of walking, always being on the move, and never settling down in one place long enough to risk being found. I walked the city in endless circles throughout my days, never spending too long in one place so as not to draw the attention of the cops. I never knew how far and wide Greg's operation ran, but I knew there were cops in his back pocket. Bribed with money, drugs, and women. That was made clear the first time Greg beat me within an inch of my life, and they came to arrest me at the hospital instead of him. 'Self-defense,' he said while sporting busted knuckles. He dragged me back home after a twenty-four-hour lock-up, telling me I was lucky and that I should thank him for bailing me out. *Fucking asshole*. Why did I only shoot him in the kneecap again?

I grumble to myself as I continue my trek. Water, shelter, food. They're my priorities. My mouth and throat feel dry and tender, and my breath probably stinks from the acidic bile I coughed up. I'm dying for a drink, but I'll be for-real-dead if I don't find fresh water. I can feel blisters forming on the backs of my ankles. Even my well-worn boots won't protect my feet when it comes to the friction of damp socks rubbing against my skin. I try not to think about how uncomfortable I am. I can do uncomfortable. For years, every day of my existence was uncomfortable. Instead, I focus on the shock and pain on Greg's face when I blew his kneecap out. Face twisted with rage while he sat cradling his leg, unable to move. Unable to come after me.

I really should've killed that asshole. I probably wouldn't be here right now if I had. I could be on a proper beach sipping a margarita and watching the sunset instead of sweating my tits off trying to find water and somewhere to sleep. I snort. It's not much different to what life is like on the run. At least the view is nicer. Besides, no one is actively chasing me down. If it stays that way, it'll be a relief not to have to look over my shoulder all the time or have my heart leap out of my chest every time a car backfires. This might have worked out in my favor. I can't help the smile that creeps across my face knowing that Greg will probably never find me here. For the first time in forever, I might be safe.

3

KATIE

The dark cave I stumble upon is a blessing from the heat, giving my abused feet and sweat-slicked body a chance to sit and rest. I tentatively check it for wild animals, finding it clear, but I don't dare take my boots off, just in case. I don't think I'd be able to bring myself to put them back on my aching feet if I did. I tell myself I'll only sit for a short while, just enough to catch my breath and cool down.

Mustiness from damp rocks and moss seeps from the cave, and I'm hopeful it means there's water close by. My thirst pushes me back onto my feet with a groan, and I venture further into the darkness of the cave, desperate for something cool on my tongue. I'd almost lick the moisture right off the walls. I trace my hands along the cool walls until I find a narrow opening tucked away at the back of the cave, anything beyond it obscured in darkness. I bite at my lip, catching a tab of dried skin and pulling it off. I'll take a quick look, and if there's no water, I'll turn around and come straight back.

Not taking my hand off the wall, I shuffle forward in small increments, scared the floor will disappear from beneath me as if it's a booby-trapped tunnel. In the dark and silence, the sound of my pulse in my ears and my ragged breath is amplified. Specks of phosphorescent blue appear along the ceiling, and it takes me a moment to realize they're glow worms. The clusters grow the deeper I travel, until I can trace the outline of the tunnel walls. The walls press in on me, and I decide to turn back around, disappointed at not having found the water source. It takes me two painstakingly long minutes to realize that, at some point, I must've gotten turned around in the dark, and now I'm lost.

It's okay. Don't panic. It's okay. Don't panic. I repeat it like a mantra, if only to keep my feet moving forward. It takes me a lot longer to realize I'm being followed. What I mistake for my heart thumping in my ears, thanks to the probable concussion and the spiking anxiety from being lost in the dark, is footsteps. Heavy footsteps, given the way the ground thumps beneath me with each one. A million racing thoughts spring to life, the loudest being: *the lizard monsters have changed their mind and somehow tracked me inside the cave.* Fear comes thick and fast, and I dig my hand into my pocket to ground myself with the smooth shell of my pocketknife. I have two options at my disposal. I can stay put and hope they don't cross my path, or I can run and hope like hell I don't cross theirs.

I run. What can I say? You can take the girl out of the streets, but you can't take the streets out of the girl.

My boots pound against the dark, damp stone floor as I slide around twists and turns. Tunnel walls close in on me from all sides. Clusters of glow worms light my way. The dim light casts every ridge along the stone walls in ominous shadows, causing me to jump at every noise. I curse.

I bounce off the wall as I come around a corner too fast, using the momentum to push off and propel me forward, my boots slipping beneath me. The footsteps that follow remain constant, steady. They don't increase in pace with my own, and somehow, that unnerves me more. I suddenly feel like a mouse in a trap about to be pounced on by a fat house cat with all the time in the world; just patiently waiting for me to make a misstep or to round the wrong corner right into its waiting jaws. I know I won't be able to run forever. Fatigue nips at me already from the day's walk. The heat, thirst, hunger, and blisters have already done half of the stalkers' job for them. All they have to do is wait for me to get tired or for an injury to take me down. An easy meal, handed to them on a silver platter.

I swat my bangs away from my forehead, sweat stinging my eyes as I squint into the darkness, expecting to see glowing eyes staring back at me. I rest for a moment, bent over with my hands braced upon my knees as I attempt to take in more air. I'm fading fast. It's only a matter of time before they catch me, but I won't go down without a fight. Never again.

The footsteps continue, becoming louder the closer they get to my position. I flick the blade out, the silver steel catching the light from the glow worms. I can't run anymore, but I don't stop. Instead, I keep a steady walking pace in what I hope is the direction away from my stalkers. If not for the vibrations of their own footsteps, I would think I was now alone. I take a left, then a right, turn around at a dead end, and take the left instead, slowly making my way further into the depths beneath the mountain. The air gets warmer and wetter, moisture clinging to my skin and the walls in a light slick. I stick my tongue out, hoping to wring out a single droplet of moisture from the air. Anything to slake my thirst.

The warmth begins to be too much, paired with my exhaustion. I remove my denim jacket and discard it at my feet, looking back at it forlornly as I continue. If I make it back this way, I'll grab it on my way through, but deep down, I know I'll probably never see it again. A few more twists and turns, and a high *ting* sings out amidst the darkness. I pause, holding my breath to hear it better.

Drip, drip, drip. Water. It must be.

The idea of a sip of water, even musty cave water, is enough to get me to pick up the pace, pausing every so often to listen to the dripping, making sure I'm still heading in the right direction. I round a corner only for the tunnel to open into a large cavern. The ceiling is littered with glow worms, casting the entire space in an eerie blue glow. Warm air fogs around me while I scan the space for the single thing I'm looking for. I quickly cross the cavern to the steady dripping of water from a stalactite that reaches toward the floor, directly above a hot spring. *Jackpot.*

I drop to my knees at the edge of the spring, the stone unforgiving beneath me, and dunk my entire head into the warm pool of water. I let out a sigh of relief as I come up for air, my sopping bangs dripping water into my eyes. It's as equally satisfying as it is unsatisfying in that it's warm, but it still feels nice to wash away the sweat and sand from my face. I pool my hands in the water and bring them to my mouth, taking a big gulp, letting water run down my chin. There are probably rules about drinking hot spring water, but I can't bring myself to care.

A roar sounds off, much too close for my liking. I brace myself, the stone slick with condensation beneath my fingers, until it suddenly trembles, jolting me from my reprieve. Pebbles dance across the floor in a staccato beat, too quickly for the lazy pace of my hunters. I feel the blood drain from my face; I've been in here for too long already. Have they realized how close they are to their prey? I hasten back to the entrance of the cavern and peer around the corner. Shadows dance across the walls, yet one alone steadily draws longer the closer they get. I don't think I can create enough distance between us with them so close, at least not without them hearing. I look back over my shoulder at the warm pool nestled on the floor of the cavern. I'd have to time it right, but I think I have a plan.

4

ASTERION

A rodent of some kind has gotten trapped in the labyrinth. Again. I snort in agitation, lifting my muzzle to the air. The foreign smell reaches my nostrils all the way to my home in the center of the labyrinth.

"It better not be a rat," I grumble mostly to myself, turning away from my vegetable garden to set my watering shell to the side. The island is always listening, though.

The last time a rat found its way this deep into the labyrinth, I was overrun with the flea-infested devils before I even realized. They destroyed what little fruit and vegetables I had grown down here and shit in every crevice of my home. The only positive thing was that after I caught each one of them, I had flame-grilled rats for supper for weeks after.

I stomp out of the small vegetable patch and head into the tunnels to flush out whatever it might be. I really hope it is a rabbit. That would make a tasty stew paired with the potatoes I have grown.

Using my muzzle to guide me, I sniff around twists and turns. I could walk this labyrinth with my eyes closed, and I am surprised I have not come upon the animal quivering in a corner somewhere. Perhaps it is a clever little rabbit. It will be more satisfying when I catch it.

I tilt my head at the sound of soft footsteps and the smell of the sea and sand, edged with something sweet, drifting through the tunnels. Surely it is not a gull that has weaved its way this deep beneath the mountain. No matter. Gull stew will taste just as good as rabbit stew. Perhaps I will use a sprig of thyme, a little sea salt to bring out the taste of the bird meat, and I believe I have some lemons left from the orchard above. I salivate at the idea of a delicious meal as I continue to follow my senses, all on high alert, through the winding maze. Glow worms light my way despite being able to see perfectly well in the dark after having spent a millennium amongst it.

I round a corner, almost tripping over a rag left right in the middle of the path when it tangles around my feet. I grunt, picking up the dark, crusty cloth between two fingers, and hold it in the air in front of me. Turning it each way, I cannot make heads nor tails of it. Where did it come from? Whose is it? What is it? Bringing it to my muzzle, I inhale deeply, sniffing past the surface scents of the sand and sea to the barely there scent of strawberries and something richer beneath. Pulling back, I eye the cloth distrustfully. It reminds me of spring; of perfumed gardens overflowing with fruit, and fucking. Why would this abandoned piece of cloth smell like the things I long for? I bring it back to my face and bury my nose in the stiff material. My vision brightens when the scent fills my lungs again, as if someone has peeled back the dirt above us to let the sunshine down. My cock hardens, the length protruding from beneath my loincloth, the knot at its base taut and aching. My fist finds its way around my knot, gripping tightly, and before I can comprehend what I am doing, I come with a bellow and the scent of strawberries in my nostrils.

My seed spurts onto my loincloth and the cave floor. I stare at it in shock, disgusted at the complete and utter lack of self-control I just exhibited, and thankful there is no one to see my shame painted on the floor. The scent still lingers in my nose as I clean up my mess with the discarded rag. I throw it back where I found it, then hesitate, overcome with a possessive need to take it. Turning back, I swipe it off the stone floor with a grunt. The instinct does not make sense to me, and yet I cannot let it go. It is as if all sense has left my body.

Returning to the task at hand, I scent the air for my prey, pretending as if nothing has happened despite the seed-soaked cloth bunched tight in my fist. The ground beneath me trembles with each pounding step I take, my pace increasing as my frustration peaks. At myself, or at the little rabbit hiding in my den, I do not know, nor do I wish to inspect my feelings so closely.

We are close to my bathing chambers, the scent of my prey intensifying as I draw nearer. My pulse thrums beneath my skin in anticipation of the hunt; the chase that will ensue before I snap that little rabbit's neck. I roll my shoulders, loosening the tension that has settled there, and slip around the corner.

Mist hangs in the humid air of the dimly lit cavern, slicking the stone floor and walls with condensation. The steady drip of water from the tip of a stalactite above the hot spring is the only sound to break the silence as each drop hits the surface. There is no scuttling of rats or clicking of a gull's nails against the stone. Not even the thumping of little rabbit feet. I huff in annoyance, turning to leave my bathing chambers to continue the hunt, despite my certainty that the rodent is *here,* somewhere.

A faint pop echoes out amongst the silence. *Pop, pop, pop.*

I turn toward the noise, bubbles rising and bursting on the surface of the previously still hot spring. Steam billows from my nostrils as I approach on silent footsteps. A flash of white in the water catches my eye. Has the rabbit fallen in?

"Not so clever, then."

A snort of annoyance leaves me as I reach into the hot spring, grabbing a fistful of the rabbit's fur and yanking it out of the water. It is much heavier than I anticipated, and I must drop the seed-covered rag at my feet so I can use both hands. Something wraps around my wrist as its head breaks the surface.

A girl clings to my arm, writhing and thrashing as my fingers grip the fabric of her shirt, a look of fury on her face. Rotten strawberries assault my nose as she squawks at me, her voice high and thin, laced with an undercurrent of panic, but I do not understand the words. Short legs swing out, water spraying out in an arc as a hard foot connects with my gut. I let out a huff of air as I let the fabric go, leaving her dangling from my forearm in an attempt not to fall.

Her kick unbalances us, and I stumble over the edge, following the girl as we tip into the water. At the last minute, I twist so that we hit the water side by side in a bid to avoid falling on her. Limbs tangle as the warmth engulfs us. Another hard kick, this time to my ribs, as the girl uses my body to push herself toward the surface. I growl. Petty instinct has me reaching out to grab her ankle, pulling her back under right as her head breaks the surface with a gasp.

I stand, water dripping from my horns and snout, my fur soaked through to my skin. The spring barely reaches my chest, yet the girl seems to be struggling to reach the surface, her clothing and wickedly hard feet waterlogged. I have no idea how this small human managed to find her way here, let alone inside my labyrinth, but I suppose I cannot let her drown. I reach down, hands encircling a frame that seems so frail I could snap her in half by mere accident and throw her over my shoulder. She lets out a yelp followed by coughing as her stomach makes contact with my shoulder. I huff, payback for that sharp kick. She wriggles in my grip as I step out of the hot spring, water pooling beneath my feet.

"Let me go!" The small girl flails and grunts under my grip.

Burning sears between my shoulder blades, and I bellow, dropping the girl on the wet stone. Air escapes her with a whoosh on impact. I spin, my arms trying to reach the spot on my back from which the pain resonates, but I cannot reach it.

"What did you do?" I growl, rounding on her as she scuttles backwards on her hands and feet.

Her bottom lip trembles, and she looks no more than a child at that moment. I take a deep breath to calm the building rage inside me.

"What did you do?" I bite out.

"I st-tabbed you."

"You stabbed me," I deadpan, struggling to believe this slip of a human *stabbed* me.

She nods frantically.

"Take. It. Out," I growl, my voice low and gravelly.

I give her my back, confident that she is scared enough to obey. Wet, shaking hands touch the heat of my skin, before another slice of pain as she removes the knife from between my shoulder blades.

I turn sharply with a hiss. Her hand is poised in front of her, ready to strike me again, the small blade in her hand dripping crimson with my blood. I grab her wrist with a snort, hot air billowing in her face as I yank her toward me. The blade falls to the stone with a clatter as I bend to meet her. Glaring at her pale skin, soggy strands of violet hair stuck to her face, and big brown eyes, her scent hits me. I press my snout against the crook of her neck, inhaling her. *Strawberries.*

I push her away from me in disgust, and she stumbles.

"A little rabbit." I grunt. "More like a fucking viper."

And my mate.

5

KATIE

A viper, he called me. I feel a small sense of smugness beneath the adrenaline coursing through my veins. That's right, I *am* a viper, and I'll stab him again if I get another chance. My hand slowly reaches out to the knife that lies discarded on the stone floor near where I fell when he shoved me, right after he *sniffed* me. What is with that, anyway?

"Y-you can talk?" I try to hide the wobble in my voice while I distract him from my wandering hand. If he suspects I'm going for the knife again, I'll be for-sure-dead. He glares at me and clenches his fists at his side, and I am acutely aware of how large they are. Easily the size of my head. He could likely snap my neck without even breaking a sweat.

There are more monsters here than I originally thought. This one, however, is different from the others. He towers over me with thick arms and legs covered in a short layer of golden-brown fur. The only clothing he wears is a loincloth around his waist, exposing the rippling muscles of his stomach and the gold rings through each of his nipples. My hands tremble in fear, and I squeeze them tight, willing them to stop. The only thing more disconcerting than a monster with nipple rings is that his very buff human-like body morphs into a very inhuman-like head. A thick snout, complete with a golden nose ring to match, horns that curl above his head, dark-brown eyes, and more golden rings in his ears. The fur that covers his entire body is darkened with water, slicking it tight to his skin.

"Well, I did not moo," he growls at me, and I flinch, the reaction an involuntary habit. As much as I try to be brave, I don't think I'll ever lose that.

"How come I can understand you, when I couldn't understand those lizard monsters?" I swallow thickly, unsure if it's a nervous sweat that trickles down the side of my face or the remnants of water in my hair.

My fingers wrap around the hilt of my pocketknife, and I clench it tightly. The beast cocks his head to the side, and I think he's spotted the knife in my hand.

"The spring." He grunts, tilting his head toward the hot spring on the floor.

"Ah, yes. The spring. That explains everything. How silly of me," I mutter, deadpan.

Ignoring me, he continues, his voice rising in a growl. "You speak of the Drakons. Is this some sort of joke to them? They thought to dump you like a lost little rabbit in my labyrinth, hoping I would hunt you down, and what? Kill you? Eat you?" He begins to pace in front of me, his fists clenched at his sides. Steam rises from his nostrils the angrier he gets.

Hang on a minute, I don't like the sound of that last part. I thought I had avoided being the lizard monsters'—Drakons'—meal, and now it looks like I'm right back at square one.

He stops in front of me and snarls in my face. "Do they know you are my *mate*?"

I flinch away from him. Actually, you know what? Kill me and eat me. Being a mate, whatever that is, sounds way worse.

Not one to waste an opportunity of having him so close, I swipe at him with the knife, a thin pink gash opening on his cheek.

"WOULD YOU STOP TRYING TO STAB ME!" he roars, grabbing my wrist and yanking me to my feet, my toes scrabbling on the stone as he holds me just shy of being able to find purchase.

"Put me down!" I whimper back at him, trying to pull my arm free from his iron-like hold. "You're hurting me!"

"You *stabbed* me! Twice! Do you know what I do with snakes that bite?" His voice is dangerously low. Goose pimples prickle along my skin. "I snap them in half and eat them for dinner."

"I won't let you eat me!" I screech, twisting and kicking with all my might against this beast.

He snorts, as if me being able to stop him from doing anything is a ridiculous concept, but he lets me drop to the ground.

"Then do not give me a reason to."

He's right in my face again, brown eyes glittering like gold under the twinkling glow-worms. I gulp. Twice, I've been thwarted now. The next time I try it, I'll make sure he doesn't see it coming. I fold the knife away, slip it in my pocket, and raise my hands in surrender.

"Fine," I grumble. "I won't stab you, and you won't eat me. How's that?"

He snorts in what I assume is acceptance of my offer.

We both eye each other warily as I nurse my aching and abused wrist while he fingers the slice across his cheek.

"Dip your wrist in the spring. It will heal you." He nods to my wrist, then looks away quickly, avoiding eye contact. It's almost as if he feels guilty about hurting me. The thought makes me snort. Yeah, right. He's probably mad about not taking the opportunity to 'snap it in half'.

A magically translating and healing hot pool is about as believable as the monsters walking around, so of course, I do as he says. I kneel on the edge of the stone and lean over, dipping my wrist in the warm water. The ache fades away on a sigh, the angry red skin turning pink and then pale again. The beast also steps into the hot spring and submerges his back, healing the knife wound there. We don't let each other out of our sights, like a lion and an antelope settling on an uneasy truce to drink at the same watering hole. I tense, my body coiled tight like a spring. He splashes his face with warm water, the pink line on his cheek sealing itself back together. As soon as the water hits his face, I'm up and running.

I hear him bellow and curse, but it's too late. The cavern is already behind me.

I feel a lot better after my dip in the hot spring, despite having wet clothes again. At least this time they're not crusted and stiff with sand. The ground beneath me rumbles as the beast gives chase.

"Fuck, fuck, fuck," I mutter between panting breaths as my feet pound in time with my heartbeat. The tunnel to my right is lighter than the tunnel on my left, and I swerve down that path, hoping I've found my way back to the cave opening I began at.

As I breach the entrance, I find myself in a large cavern, the rocky ceiling forming a dome high above me, littered with so many glow worms it's as if someone has turned on a light switch. I skid to a halt, partly in awe and shock at the sudden change, blinking away the black spots that dance in my vision. When I can see clearly, I notice a rustic mud-brick hut at the center of the cavern. A doorway and window have been carved out of the wall, revealing the inside to be dark and empty of its occupants. Or should I say *occupant*, as I realize exactly who lives here. Beside the hut, a small vegetable garden sits with trellises standing tall, green vines wrapped around them and flowing over the edge of their containment.

I approach the garden, my fingers tracing over prickly leaves as I walk around it. The monster gardens? It's a curious realization that the big, scary beast seems to be domesticated enough to keep a home and garden and is not just some monster who sleeps on the floor in a dank cave somewhere. It's as if my thoughts summon him as he comes barreling through the same tunnel I vacated only moments prior, interrupting my pondering about what sort of being he is as he charges directly for me, bent at the waist, his horns aimed for my throat.

With a squeak, I scramble for an exit and am met with at least twenty of them lining the walls of the cavern. Which one do I pick? I spin in circles, panic clouding any decision-making skills I have. Before I can decide, the beast collides with my body, and it feels like I've been hit by a car. My breath escapes in a gasp upon impact before I hit the ground front on, strong arms banded around my face and body to protect me from the worst of it. His nose is tucked in the crook of my neck, his horns buried into the dirt floor on either side of my head. I freeze in shock, with his body pressed firmly against my back, our heavy pants mingling.

"Do. *Not.* Move." His breath is ragged and hot against my cheek as he bites out the words.

I'm trapped in this cage his body has made around me. I don't think I can move even if I wanted to. I don't even have the words to protest; my brain has not yet caught up with my body. I feel something thick and hard against the back of my leg, turning my blood ice cold. The sensitive spot between my legs begins to throb.

"Is that your di—?" I begin to hiss, rubbing my thighs together from the unusually timed flood of heat that pools at my core.

"Not. Yet," he grunts out. "If you move, I will not be able to stop myself. *Please*," he pleads, pain laced around every word.

Used to obeying, I do as I'm told. I don't think I want to find out what it is he's trying to stop himself from doing. I remain frozen, both of us lying there in silence for so long, the tension melts out of our limbs. Our body heat melds us together until a thin sheen of sweat covers my skin.

He groans into my neck, the hard length twitching against my leg as he breathes in my scent.

"Why do you smell so Fates-damned good?" He bites it out like I'm doing it on purpose, but I don't know what he's talking about because, quite frankly, I stink.

6

ASTERION

A new feeling settles right behind my sternum, my heart jumping to escape its cage as my body presses against my mate's, and I know I am completely at the Fates' mercy. It is taking every ounce of me not to rut into this Fates-forsaken girl beneath me. Her strawberry scent is maddening, driving my primal instincts to the forefront, reducing my self-control to an infinitesimal blip in my consciousness. When she ran—Fates help me—there was nothing on this earth that could have stopped me from giving chase.

She squirms beneath me, and a shiver wracks my body. Every muscle aches from the tension of holding myself back. My horns throb at the base from driving them into the ground in a bid to prevent any injury to this slip of a human. I can feel the rawness of my forearms where they skidded against the dirt floor, rocky debris embedding itself in my skin. Though it is better my skin than hers.

The only mark I want to see on her milky skin is the red imprint of my hand across her backside. I grunt, annoyed at myself. These are not thoughts I should be having. This girl has already caused me more trouble in the last hour than any other has in the last millennium.

I have played right into the Drakons' dirty trick, and the loss of control sinks like a heavy rock of shame in the pit of my gut. That alone is enough to help my cock soften, and my limbs relax in a sigh of relief, glad that the adrenaline of the hunt has finally abated. The girl makes a muffled sound beneath me before slamming the back of her skull into my nose. Sharp pain radiates up its length and behind my eyes, and I roll off her, lying on my back in the dirt, my chest heaving with anger as I rub my snout.

"Why you little—" My muffled growl is cut off.

"It wasn't enough to chase me down and pin me with your giant fucking dick," she gasps out. "You had to smother me as well? Fuck."

The girl pushes up onto her hands and knees, head bowed as she catches her breath. Her dark shirt sticks to her back from our combined sweat and drapes beneath her, revealing a thin stretch of milky stomach. Thin is an understatement. She does not look like she has eaten a full meal in her life. Straggly hair hangs over her forehead in violet strands as she shoots me a dirty look. This girl has more fight in her than she has any right to. A viper indeed.

I say nothing, but she is right. Shame, shame, shame—it courses through my bloodstream, making my cheeks heat. Anger at the Drakons for using my own weaknesses against me burns in my veins. I decide that this affront cannot stand. The Drakons will take her back whether they want to or not. Mates be damned.

I heft myself back onto my feet, surprised that she has not tried to run already. She eyes me warily as she also stands, trepidation in her gaze as she slowly begins backing up upon my approach. She holds out her hands in front of her as though trying to placate a wild animal, and that makes the anger simmering inside me overflow.

"Why are you looking at me like that? We had a deal. You said you weren't going to eat me—!" She ends in a squeak as I reach her in two steps and grab her elbow. I hold her tight enough that she cannot get free, but I am also now aware of how frail her bones are, so I do not grip so tight as to cause her bruising like earlier. I pull her toward my home, making her turn and stumble after me.

"Wh-what are you doing?" Her voice wobbles, soured strawberries perfuming the air, giving away her fear.

"I am taking you back," I grunt out as we enter the small hut.

"Sit." I shove her toward a stool in the corner, concealed by shadows. I do not bother to light a candle as I throw together a pack for traveling. She watches my every move closely from her place perched on the edge of the stool, ready to take flight at a moment's notice.

I grab dried meats and herbs, some root vegetables I harvested only yesterday, a thin piece of slate to cook upon, pots, and a water skin that I fill from a spigot I rigged into the wall of my hut, pulling from the natural spring beneath the mountain. The water is lukewarm but clean enough for drinking. I also grab a flint for lighting a fire—though we should only need it for cooking. The temperature is always mild in Aeolia. Trapped in a constant state of spring, there is not often a need for additional warmth.

I do not expect the journey up the mountain to take more than a couple of nights before we reach the Drakons, but I am also used to traveling at my pace and not the pace of a girl whose legs are half the length of mine and whose body might take flight at the first sign of a stiff breeze.

"Do I get a say on whether or not I go back?" a small but haughty voice chimes out from the corner.

"No," I reply, tying the pack tight and hoisting it over my shoulder.

"Well, I guess there's nothing stopping me from running again." She shrugs, nonplussed.

I narrow my gaze at her, then look around my home until I spot what it is I am looking for. Unraveling the braided rope, I tie one end around my middle and stalk over to where she sits on the stool, her legs swinging in the air since she cannot touch the ground. The sight is ridiculous—the stool that is perfect for me makes her look even more miniature.

She looks up at me distrustfully, and I loop the other end of the rope around her middle and pull it tight before she can protest.

"Hey! What the hell!" She jumps off the stool, and I cannot help but snort, tucking the laughter away behind pursed lips. I would not want the little viper to slash me again with that wicked little blade.

I tug on the rope, jolting her toward me, and reach my fingers into the little hideaway that she has on her pants. It is so small and tight that I can only wriggle two fingers in there to retrieve the blade she has tucked away. She sucks in a sharp breath, her body coiled up and tense. Her bottom lip pops open just slightly, and I can hear the quiet unevenness of her breath. In the shadows, her pupils dilate, and the scent of strawberries wafts from her skin. *Great.* Now I am never going to get her Fates-damned scent out of my home. I retrieve the blade and tuck it away in the waistband of my loincloth.

"Would not want you cutting your way free." I grunt, swiftly turning on my heel and heading for the doorway.

"Come." I smirk, knowing that this little viper has no choice but to heed my order. I do not look at her as I leave my home, but I feel the small resistance on the rope as she hesitates for as long as she can before she stumbles after me.

7

ASTERION

"**M**otherfucker," I hear her hiss, falling into line behind me as I pull her across the dusty cavern before entering one of the tunnels without hesitation. A lifetime in these caves means I have memorized every path in this serpentine labyrinth. I know the exact tunnels I need to take to get anywhere.

"I did not 'fuck' my mother," I growl at her, shooting a glare over my shoulder as I tug the rope hard enough to make her stumble. This little wretch has a wicked tongue that strikes as viciously as a blade in her hands.

"I didn't—that's not what I meant." She stumbles over her words, brushing her hair out of her eyes.

"That was my father."

She almost chokes. "Is that how you came to be a—?"

"A Minotaur, yes."

She clears her throat. "So, was your mother a Minotaur too?"

"No."

"Your father then?"

"You talk too much."

"Just making small talk," she grumbles.

"Talk smaller." This human talks far too much and walks far too little.

"O-kay then," she mutters under her breath.

In truth, I do not know my parents outside of the stories I have been told. My mother was cursed by a God to fall in lust with a beast because my father had failed to uphold his sacrificial honor. I was only an infant when I was taken from my mother and placed inside the labyrinth. My only company, the fourteen people sent to me every nine years in sacrifice. That is, until the Fates brought us here and shielded all the monsters from the modernizing outside world.

I wind through tunnels and around corners, passing the hot spring along the way, and then, almost abruptly, we come to the cave entrance. The sun has since set, a cool breeze wafting in off the ocean, and it feels like bliss across my skin after being in the warm and stuffy underground. It is not too long a journey, but I am eager to be aboveground for a short while. It is not often that I get to see real stars scattered across the skies. The glow worms are a poor substitute for the beauty of the constellations.

I jerk. The rope anchoring the girl and me together pulls taut as I head for the crudely carved entrance. I look back at her, eyes narrowing when I see her standing behind me with her arms crossed over her chest and a defiant look in her eye.

"What are you doing?" I rumble, eyebrows furrowed in annoyance.

"Where are we going?"

I growl. "I told you."

"No, you didn't. You just said 'back'. Back where?" She narrows her eyes at me.

"To the Drakons."

"Dragons?" She squeaks. "The lizard monsters?"

"Drakons." I snort. "And yes."

I shake my head to myself. Ladon and Pytho would have something to say about being called lizards. The thought almost makes me smile.

"No." She clenches her teeth and juts her chin out.

"Yes." I pinch the bridge between my eyes. We do not have time for this.

"No."

"Yes."

"No, and I can do this all night." She sits down on the cave floor and crosses her legs.

I huff, fists clenching at my sides, before stalking over to her, my heavy footfalls making the stones rattle. In one swoop, I pick her up and sling her over my shoulder.

"Hey!" she yelps, her stomach making impact with my shoulder so that her head hangs near the middle of my back. She bangs her fists against my hardened muscles.

"Let me down!"

"No."

"Arghhh!" she screeches, and I am very glad her head is not up near my ears.

This little wisp is as light as a feather, and bony too. I do not care for the complaints she mutters as I leave the cave and begin our journey to the mountain.

The grass is long, almost to my thighs, and jagged boulders peek out in spots, making the terrain uneven. Silvery moths flit around the grass, the moonlight making their wings shimmer. I can smell the ocean still, the salt floating in on the cool breeze and mixing with the scent of strawberries that is now annoyingly too close to my nose.

"Achooo!" The girl sneezes, and sneezes, and sneezes.

"Will you pull yourself together?!" I growl, my grip around her thighs tightening with my annoyance. She squirms beneath my hold with a whimper, her scent thickening. Right along with my cock.

"Fates." I groan, running my palm down my face. At least with her head smacking against my back, she cannot see my now-erect length tenting my loincloth.

"Fates-damned mate bond," I mutter and shake my head. "Fates-damned Drakons and their tricks."

The sneezing stops, thank the Fates. "What's a mate bond?"

I almost trip, her question catching me off guard and causing me to stumble on a rock sticking out in the way of our path.

I clear my throat. "It is a bond between two souls that ties them together for eternity. Or until one of them dies, I suppose."

Now, there is a thought. Maybe I could throw her off the side of the mountain and be done with it. I grimace. Severing a mate bond is quite traumatic. After bearing witness to Cyclops and his grief, I do not wish that upon anyone, least of all myself. But I also do not want to be stuck with this little viper and her frustratingly delicious scent for the rest of eternity.

"Sounds horrible. Who would want to be stuck with someone forever?" She shudders, and the rippling of her body against my shoulder makes my loins ache.

"You have no idea." *How much I want exactly that.* But not with someone who has been used to tempt me. Perhaps I should explain to her that she is mine and I am hers, but the words do not come. I can only imagine her reaction. I pat the small knife tucked into the waist of my loincloth, checking that it is still there, despite knowing she has not had any opportunity to snatch it back. I trust the little viper as much as she weighs, which is very Fates-damned little.

My mate needs to be strong and sturdy, especially if we are to mate. I could snap this girl in half just by accident. She would need to eat a lot of food just to keep up with me. I could make her roast meats over the fire, collect the fat drippings to cook up root vegetables with.

Pressure settles low in my gut, my cock jutting straight out at the thought of feeding a mate. My mate. And then rutting into her until we are both sated and full. Full of food and full of my seed.

All I want to do is take my cock in my hand and release the pressure there, but I do not. And I should not be thinking about all the things I could cook for this little viper until her bones no longer protrude from her skin. She is probably just as likely to carve out my heart and eat it than accept anything I make for her.

The ground begins to incline, the path up the mountain a few hours ahead, and the ground rises and falls into soft hills the closer we get. My erection finally goes down, but there's a tenderness that sits inside my balls at the inability to empty themselves.

A soft snoring comes from my back, and I realize the girl has fallen asleep. I am equally impressed and annoyed that she was able to do so even while thrown over my shoulder. We will need to camp for the night and be ready to begin our ascent as the sun rises, so I find a clearing that is mostly free from sharp, pointy rocks and drop the girl to the ground, not at all being gentle with her sleeping form.

I smirk when she wakes with a startle and a yelp, rubbing her behind.

"What was that for?"

"We will make camp here tonight." I take my pack off and remove a fur, lay it on the ground, and settle upon it. She looks around us at the clearing and then back at me. I lie down and close my eyes, preparing to sleep so that I am well-rested for the journey in the morning.

"Where am I going to sleep?"

I open one eye to peer at her. She wrings her hands in front of her, and despite her aggravated tone, her hands and the souring of her scent betray her anxiety.

"I am sure right there is good enough." I gesture to the ground beneath her with a smirk.

She glowers at me before crossing her arms over her chest. "Are you not going to light a fire, at least?"

I snort and close my eyes again. "Why would I do that?"

"Uh, for warmth? To keep the wolves away? I don't know." Her annoyance brings me great pleasure.

"There is not a tree in sight to gather firewood from, and I am not going to go looking just for you to run off again." I turn over, my back now to her. I do not tell her there are no wolves on this island, however. Best to keep her scared of leaving my side, so I do not have to hunt her down again. She does not reply, though I can feel her glare searing into the back of my skull. For the first time since catching the little viper, I crack a grin, knowing she is sitting there seething at me.

"Besides, I am the scariest thing out here."

8

KATIE

Fury simmers inside me at the sheer audacity of this beast. I am more awake now that I've had a little nap, and I assess my surroundings. He's right, there are no trees. Nothing for me to hide behind in an attempt at escape. I know with this open plain, I wouldn't make it two steps before I'm tackled again. Besides, there is still the rope tying us together to be dealt with. I bristle at the reminder of him pinning me to the ground, a dull throb resuming between my thighs when I think of how I could feel his scarily large appendage against my leg. He could kill a girl with that thing, and yet I feel myself getting wetter at the thought of it, of how hard he was. Of the warmth and weight of his body against mine. It's been a few months since I've been with a man, Greg being the last, and the experience left me not desiring a repeat encounter anytime soon. So, why hasn't my body gotten the memo? This Minotaur is a beast in more ways than one, and I certainly don't want him.

I settle on the ground, clenching my thighs together in a bid to ignore the need that's made itself at home in my body. The ground is thankfully devoid of any rocks as I curl onto my side and wrap my arms around my waist to stay warm, the cold, hard dirt sucking it from me almost instantly. I'd kill to have my jacket right now, and I mentally kick myself for leaving it in the labyrinth. I stare at the Minotaur's broad expanse of back muscles, watching it rise and fall so rhythmically, I think he might be asleep already. I am so uncomfortable that I can't even think of closing my eyes. If I wait just a bit longer, I might be able to attempt to pry my knife back from the waistband of his loincloth, and then I can cut this rope and make a break for it.

I don't remember falling asleep, but as my consciousness stirs, the morning sun on my face, I feel so blissfully rested and refreshed. Then I remember I was so uncomfortable last night. Frowning, I open my eyes only to be met with a soft fur-coated chest, complete with two nipple rings, staring back at me like a pair of judging golden eyes. I tense, the illusion of being warm and cozy shattered as I question how the hell I ended up a few feet from where I settled down for the evening, and why exactly I am curled up in the arms of the Minotaur. I run a mental checklist: Not missing any clothing? Check. No body parts hurt? Check. Although the need between my thighs hasn't dissipated in the slightest. The ache is like an annoying mosquito bite I just want to scratch.

Relief that nothing untoward seems to have happened to me in my unconscious state floods through my body, and I relax a little. The warm fur beneath me does a surprisingly good job of cushioning against the ground, and I'm incredibly comfortable despite being exposed to the elements. Amongst other things. I swallow thickly as I glance down the Minotaur's broad body to the only item of clothing he wears, and within it, the red glint of the knife handle peeks out. This is the perfect opportunity to get it back. I very slowly reach down to wiggle it out without waking him. I get my fingertips around the end of it and give a slight pull, feeling it shift a little as I ease it out.

"Fucking hell!" I screech as I'm flattened by a thick body pinning me into the ground, my hand trapped between us in the process, and judging by the size of the thing in my grip, I no longer have a hold on my knife.

"What do you think you are doing?" the Minotaur growls into my face.

"Nothing," I squeak out, staring past the golden ring in his nose, to his golden-brown eyes that glare at me beneath him.

He hardens above me, and I am sadly not talking about his muscles. His trouser-snake, or should I say anaconda, twitches inside my fist. My mouth floods with saliva before my brain takes over, and we both roll away from each other in disgust. I wipe my hand on the leg of my jeans as we sit on the fur in silence with our backs to each other. I mentally scold myself for my body's complete inability to control itself.

Fortunately, my pocketknife slips out from between us, and I snatch it from the fur while his back is turned, sliding it back into my pocket. He clears his throat and stands up, startling me, and I try my hardest not to look like a kid caught with their hand in the cookie jar. He doesn't check to make sure the knife is still securely tucked away in his loincloth, and I relax just a little.

My eyes flick toward said loincloth. *Don't look!* I mentally chide myself. His excitement is no longer noticeable. Thankfully. I seem to be exactly eye level with it as I stare at him from the ground. I wouldn't want to have my eye poked out with that thing. In one swoop, he pulls the fur out from under me and shakes it out before rolling it back up and putting it away in his pack.

"Hey!" I protest, tumbling over until I'm in the dirt.

"Let us go, before the sun rises too high."

Without waiting for me, he promptly turns and walks off, only pausing when the rope between us pulls taut. Grumbling, I get up and dust myself off, rubbing at the marks across my middle where the rope has caused friction against my skin, a light pink line marking my stomach and sides.

I trudge along behind him in silence, not making any effort to help speed up this journey. The mountain trail doesn't seem to get used often. The ground is littered with loose rocks; the dirt has softened over time from feet traversing over the path frequently. In some places, tall strands of grass threaten to overtake it completely. My eyes water and my nose itches before a bout of sneezing overcomes me.

"Achoo, achoo, achoo, achoo!" I sigh, but it comes out more like a wheeze, and I dab my eyes and nose with the bottom of my tee.

The Minotaur looks over his shoulder at me.

"Are you well?" He looks at me like he doesn't care if I'm sick or not, his concern merely for whether I will slow him down.

"I think I might be allergic to this dust, or grass, or something—" My voice is thick with congestion.

"Allergic?"

"Makes you sneeze, and itchy. Sometimes it can cause death if it's a bad enough reaction."

"Death?" Something flickers across his gaze, and I can't help but feel like death might be the solution to all his problems. *My* death, specifically. I bristle.

"I won't die. Well, not from this. I might sneeze to death, though."

He purses his lips, pondering, then stalks back to me.

"What are you doing?" I take a few steps back, my hands up as if I can stop him from whatever he's made up his mind on. I look at the edge of the path over my shoulder. We're not that far up yet, so a fall probably wouldn't kill me, but that doesn't mean it wouldn't hurt like hell.

He grabs at my wrists, pulling me into him before bending down, scooping me up behind my legs, and throwing me over his shoulder.

"Hey! Come on!" I groan, beating his back. "This isn't going to help, you know! I'm still just as close to the grass and the dirt as I am walking on my own two feet if that's what you were hoping for."

He grunts. "Perhaps, but if I must listen to you sneeze all day, I can at least ensure our journey does not take so long." He jostles me on his shoulder to reposition my body like I'm nothing but a sack of potatoes. I should be offended, but instead I'm mildly turned on at how he can just pick me up like it's nothing. On the other hand, he could throw me around just as easily. Greg flashes through my mind. That thought quickly douses any lingering arousal from this morning.

It's not much use fighting him now that I'm hanging over his shoulder like a limp rag doll, but with each step up the mountain, I become wary of how much harder it's going to be to escape.

9

ASTERION

This ridiculous human could *die* from *grass*. Fates have mercy, why would they give me a mate that is so fragile? At one point, her scent sweetens and then abruptly sours when I throw her over my shoulder, and for some reason, that bothers me more than it should. I should not care what has caused her scent to wilt like rotten strawberries, yet it is all I can think about as I hike along the overgrown mountain path.

We continue to trek in silence, her small fits of sneezing the only noises until her stomach takes up gurgling next to my ear. When I can no longer ignore it, I find a section of path wide enough for us to sit and rest on. I drop her down off my shoulder unceremoniously, hearing her growl of protest as she lands on her behind in the dirt.

"You couldn't set me on my feet?" She glowers at me.

"Why would I do that when this is more satisfying?" I snort, dumping the pack at my feet before rifling through it for some of the dried meat and the skin of water, thrusting them into her lap. "Eat."

She looks as if she might argue with me, but her stomach growls again, and she closes her mouth as her cheeks turn pink. I hum to myself as I watch her take a bite of the dried meat, and satisfaction at seeing her eat something I have made with my own hands courses through me. I take a bite myself, keeping my eyes on her as she takes a sip of water, a trickle of it escaping her lips and running down her chin. The dried meat turns gluggy in my mouth as my saliva dries up, my eyes focused on that bead of water on her skin. Heat fills my core, and I fight the urge to lean over and swipe it away with my tongue.

"What are you looking at?" She wipes her chin with her shirt and glares at me. I force myself to swallow, shaking my head to loosen up some sense. The mate bond is causing all sorts of chaos, my mind and body completely at odds with one another.

I do not answer her; instead, I snatch back the water skin and the remainder of the dried meat and pack them away.

"Hey! I wasn't done!"

I almost give in and hand it back to her. Filled with the need to see her belly full and sated like any real mate of mine should be. But I hold fast, slinging the pack back over my shoulder.

"Up." I gesture to my shoulder.

"Nah-uh. No more. I'll walk." She folds her arms across her chest where she sits on the ground.

"You are too slow. It will take us twice as long."

"Oh no, that would be such a shame—" An eyebrow disappears behind the violet hair that falls to her eyes. She tries to hide the hint of a smirk at the possibility of making the journey more difficult than necessary.

"I wish to be rid of you as soon as possible."

I tug at the rope binding us together to get her to stand. She lets out a hiss, quickly getting to her feet. The motion reveals where the rope has rubbed her skin raw, the milky white of her stomach now tinted with a pink line where it has sat around her middle. I take two steps toward her, grabbing her around her biceps and spinning her to check the skin of her back as well. She gasps as I lift her shirt, the skin there redder and more tender than the rest. I place a hand against the mark, feeling the heat emanating from it. A deep grumble rolls through me. She risks an infection if this continues to get any worse, and as much as I absolutely want to be rid of her, I cannot bring myself to cause her more harm. I should not care, but I am not a monster despite what she might think, even if I should wear the face of one. Do I untie her and risk her escaping?

"Fates," I curse under my breath, tearing a long strip of fabric from my loincloth and wetting it with water from the skin.

"What are you doing?" she asks over her shoulder as I reach around her to untie the rope that binds us together, the scent of her in my nose again as I step in close.

I grab the wet strip of cloth and begin carefully wrapping it around her middle. She lets out a hiss and grabs my wrist to halt me when the cold cloth touches the rawness of her wounds. We both tense at the contact, eyes meeting in a flick of surprise before we both pull away, and pink creeps up the sides of her neck to stain her cheeks. The physical contact ignites the mate bond inside me, heat unfurling low in my gut.

I clear my throat. "I need to tie it off." I gesture to the ends hanging loose at her sides.

"I can do it." She steps away from me, tying the cloth herself. One step separates us, and yet the distance feels like the span of the universe. We are but two planets unbalanced and adrift. One touch and I have been tipped off my axis.

I pick up the abandoned rope from the ground, one end still securely tied around my waist, and contemplate my choices. I can let her walk freely and trust that she will remain at my side, or I can choose the opposite, securing her to me once more.

She cocks that pesky eyebrow while she watches me weigh my decisions. I close the distance between us, looping the rope around her wrist and securing it with a knot. Her face instantly falls, replaced with a glower so deadly it could cut.

"Shall we then?" she snaps, tugging the tie at her wrist. She turns on her heel and storms off, continuing her way up the mountain until the rope pulls taut.

"Are you coming or not?" Her words are sharp as she stands ahead of me with her hands planted on her hips, chin pointed high.

"I don't want to be stuck here with you any more than you want to be stuck with me."

Good, I think. We are at least on the same page. Perhaps I was too hasty in my decision to tie her back up, but it is done now. I will take her back to the Drakons, and she will no longer be my problem.

"Well? We don't have all day."

I nod, more to myself than anything, satisfied with my plan to continue. She takes that as my agreement and turns her back to me before storming off as I follow along behind her. I am quick to catch up when one of my steps is two of hers. However, I do not miss the way her fists clench at her sides. She is furious at me, as she should be. I have only caused her harm thus far, and I have no intention of doing anything otherwise, mate be damned. I rub at my sternum and try to ignore the tender ache that has formed there.

I do not want a mate, and I especially do not want her.

10

Katie

My mind swirls as I storm up the mountain. How is it possible for him to be caring one moment, and then horrible again the next? His demeanor changes so fast, I get whiplash. While I also don't want to be stuck with him forever—mates? No, thank you—I also don't want to be handed over to the Drakons. There's no telling what they would do with me, and besides being tackled that one time, the Minotaur has shown no intention of eating me for dinner. Better the enemy you know than the one you don't.

I ponder a plan while we hike in silence, with me leading the way. It takes every fiber of my being not to look over my shoulder at him. Not that I need to. I can feel his dominating presence behind me, his shadow smothering my own as the sun begins its decline for the day. The higher we get, the more my chances of escaping dwindle. I'm more likely to trip and fall over the edge of the mountain than get away successfully. In my anger at being tied to him again, I inadvertently cut myself off from an escape path when I stormed ahead, putting the Minotaur at my back, allowing him to quite easily block the route back down.

I curse silently. Perhaps I'm going about this the wrong way. Do I want a mate? No. Do I even know what that means? Also, no. But I'm not going back home, and I'm not going to just let myself be handed over to a pair of overgrown lizards. I've gotten myself out of stickier situations, and I can do it again. I graze my hand over the thin bulge in my pocket where my knife is safely tucked away. If I can just get him to let his guard down, I might be able to distract him and get away, or even sneak away in the night. I just need to get free of this rope around my wrist first.

"If I promise to not run away, will you untie me?" I sling over my shoulder.

"No."

Well, it was worth asking. Initiate plan B—Operation Befriend the Beast—and hope he finds it somewhere in that big chest of his to let me go.

"What's your name?" I ask.

"My name?" His voice is gravelly and rough, the sound of it skitters down my back. If he weren't my captor and a giant pain in the ass, there's a very small part of me that wonders what that voice might sound like saying other things.

"I can't exactly keep calling you Beast, or Minotaur, can I?" I do look over my shoulder at him this time. Technically, I can call him whatever I want, but in the name of our pretend friendship, I should learn his name. Especially if I want my act to be believable.

"Why should we learn each other's names when I intend to be rid of you?"

Well, fuck. He's going to be harder to crack than I thought. Stubborn beast. Minotaur. UGH.

"Have it your way then," I snap. *Friendly.* I'm supposed to be friendly. Though he certainly doesn't make it easy. I stomp my way up the mountain, as far away from him as the rope will allow before it pulls tight between us. Initiate plan C—quietly saw at the rope with my knife and hope he doesn't notice. I will begin tonight when he sleeps.

The sky turns dusky pink and orange as the sun continues its descent. A chill sweeps up the mountain, swirling around us, my hair catching in my mouth as I puff and pant along the path that seems to wind its way upwards in a never-ending climb. Shrubbery becomes sparse the higher we travel, our surroundings succumbing to spindly brush and jagged rocks as far as the eye can see. A shiver takes me, goose pimples spreading across my arms as the temperature dips with the oncoming darkness. I cross my arms over myself, rubbing at my biceps, my tee doing nothing to buffer the chill, and I dread another night of sleeping on the hard ground.

"We should camp here for the night." The Minotaur catches up to me easily, another uneasy reminder that I need to plan my escape carefully. He's at least a foot or two taller than me, his legs much longer than mine, and he closes the distance I put between us in just a few steps. I huff, sitting down right where I stand, bringing my knees to my chest and wrapping my arms around them in a bid to trap some warmth between my lack of layers. The Minotaur crouches beside me, removing his pack and fishing inside it before taking out a couple of sharp-looking rocks.

I scrunch my face up. "Why would you pack rocks? Is there not enough around to your liking?" I tease, as he snaps off a couple of branches and leaf litter from some brush next to us and piles it in a heap at our feet. He snorts, and I think it might have almost been a laugh.

"Are you laughing at me?"

"They are not just any rocks. They are flint rocks." He starts striking them against one another above the collection of debris. I watch closely, confused as to what it is he's trying to achieve when he strikes them again, causing a spark to appear and ignite the pile of branches and leaf litter. He leans over the lightly smoldering bundle with his hands cupped around the smoke to protect it from the breeze and gently blows on it until a flame catches.

"Oh!" I gasp. A fire, thank goodness. "Can you show me how to do that?" It would be a useful skill to know if I plan to make it out here on my own.

He looks at me, shocked. "You cannot make fire?"

"Uh, no. We have houses and heating, and when we don't have those, we have lighters and matches to make fires."

He grumbles something under his breath that sounds a lot like 'useless mate' and something about 'Fates' that makes me bristle. He may think I'm useless, but I haven't survived on the run and on the streets for the past few months without learning a trick or two. It may not be quite as simple as using matches or a lighter, but I'm certain I can figure it out.

I snatch the flint from his hands and make my own little pile of leaves and sticks while he gently fans at his, feeding it some bigger branches until it's glowing a healthy orange. The fire warms my exposed limbs, and I let out a sigh of contentment as my body unwinds the tension that has settled in my bones after walking all day. I practice striking the rocks together. They make a clacking sound on impact but don't create any sparks. I grit my teeth together and try again, and again, and again.

The Minotaur produces a pot made from hardened clay. I eye it curiously, pausing my fire-making attempts. It looks as if it was made by hand; roughly shaped and uneven, but it holds the water he fills it with from the skin just fine. He adds some strips of dried meat, some greens, wilted from being stuffed in the pack, and a couple of baby potatoes to the mix before placing it on top of his fire. I turn back to my pile of branches and strike again. The smell from the simmering stew reaches me, wafting on thin tendrils of steam, making my mouth water. Groaning, I turn back to the flint. I strike again. And again.

The sun is almost fully set for the evening, the sky now a mixture of purples and deep blues. The fire casts us both in a warm orange glow that flickers with the dancing flames, little red sparks floating off above us on the breeze to the sounds of crackles and pops. Beads of sweat form above my top lip and between my breasts, whether it's from the fire or from how hard I'm concentrating, I don't know. I huff, blowing my fringe up and off my forehead where it's begun to stick. At least I won't be cold tonight when it's time to sleep.

"Argh!" I curse, tossing the flints to the dirt after my millionth attempt to get this damn fire to light, and the Minotaur rolls his eyes at me. He moves to sit behind me, his arms and legs bracketing me on both sides.

"What are you doing?" All the muscles in my body tense as I flinch, wrapped up in his oversized frame.

"It is painful to watch you. I am putting us both out of our misery."

He picks the flint stones back up and places them in my hands, moving them subtly into the correct position. Holding my wrists, he moves my arms for me, bringing my hands together for the stones to smack against each other. His chest presses against my back, adding to the heat from the fire at my side. Sweat trickles down my spine. His nose hangs over my shoulder, and the sound of him breathing in my ear is slow and steady. The flint doesn't spark.

I am very aware of how close we are to one another. How he smells like freshly turned soil after a storm and a wood fire like the one currently burning. It reminds me of camping as a child, and roasting marshmallows, of telling ghost stories by torchlight in our tents while lightning strikes outside. Happy memories. Perhaps the happiest memories I have. I close my eyes, letting myself breathe him in, soaking in his warmth. I don't resist as I feel his head dip closer to my shoulder, and he brings my hands together again to strike the stones. I open my eyes right as a spark springs to life, jumping from the stones to the dried-up leaves and twigs. I squeal, dropping the flints to clap my hands at my success, the Minotaur having let me go.

"Now, gently blow on the ember to get it to ignite." His voice is barely above a whisper, and if he wasn't right beside my head, I might not have even heard him. I lean forward, cupping my hands around the little glow like I remember seeing him do. Big tawny hands come up near my face, pulling my hair back over my shoulders and holding it at bay as I blow, gently coaxing the little ember into a small flame. It catches. The flames start small, eating away at all the dead wood until the fire is alive and wild.

I twist to grin in triumph at the Minotaur, my hair tumbling loose from his grip where he kept it from catching alight. He stares back at me, flames dancing in his golden eyes, his face contorted as if in pain. His hand is still midair, so close to my face that if he moved just the slightest, he would be touching my cheek in a caress. My grin falters, and my mouth dries up, wondering what it is he could be thinking about that has him looking at me like that. Firelight makes our shadows flicker against the mountain wall. It turns the thin coating of fur over his skin into a luxurious caramel. For the first time since being caught, I think to myself that the Minotaur might just be handsome, if he wasn't such an ass.

11

ASTERION

I thought she would have given up in her attempt to learn how to use the flint stones a lot sooner than she did. But given her stubbornness in every other aspect, I should not have been surprised that she did not. When I thought I could not take the sound of the stones smacking against each other one more time, she finally gave up.

I must admit that I was impressed by her willingness to learn and took pity on her inability to get it to work, having kept my mouth shut when she held one of the flints the wrong way around. I knew it was never going to light from the beginning of her efforts. Perhaps it was cruel to let her continue to try, knowing it would not light, because despite my keen dislike of the little viper, I cannot bear the disheartened look on her face as she stares at the stones she discarded.

I did not intend to help her, but my body moves before I realize what I am doing. Knowing that my stew bubbles away happily on my own fire, I settle in behind her, picking the stones back up and placing them in her hands the right way around before showing her the correct way to smack them together. The proximity of her body, her warmth, the smell of strawberries mixed with something decadent is not lost on me. So distracted am I by the intensity of the mate bond flaring to life in my chest that I hit the stones at the wrong angle. Disgruntled at the effect her scent has on me, I try again.

I lean further into her, as if my body has a mind of its own, sensing the nearness of my mate and demanding we be closer. Her rich strawberry smell almost makes me dizzy as it fills my nose, her contentment from the warmth increasing the intensity of it tenfold. I attempt to stifle my breathing, taking short, shallow breaths to avoid inhaling so much of her. The last thing I want is to be so overcome with the mate bond that I do something I regret. *Concentrate.*

I strike the flints against one another, and this time a spark ignites, settling itself amongst her small pile of debris. She follows my instructions, leaning forward to gently blow on the ember, and without thinking, my hands brush her violet strands of hair away from the flame, pulling them over her shoulder into a little twist around my fist.

I cannot take my eyes away from those strands of hair twirling between my fingers. The mate bond angrily stirs low in my gut, and I can already feel my cock hardening between us. How sweet this hair would look twisted in the grip of my hand while I filled my mate with my knot and my seed until it ran down the backs of her legs.

But she cannot be my mate. She is too small, too weak. The consequence of a poorly enacted trick by the Drakons.

She turns to me, her face alight and triumphant that we got it to work. I force myself to relax my grip on her hair, and silken strands slide through my fingers. Fingers that are now a hairsbreadth away from the flushed skin of her cheek. I could reach out and touch her, caress her face in the palm of my hand. I could lean in and swipe the perspiration beading on her skin with a flick of my tongue. My eyes are transfixed on a bead that trails down her neck and into her shirt. I wonder if she tastes like strawberries, too.

My cock is painfully hard, and if she notices, she does not mention it. I try to think of anything else to get it to go down—rotten oysters, that one time the latrine blocked, rodents in my vegetable garden. At last, it softens, and I quickly move away from her, back to my own fire, where my stew smells as if it is ready. I remove it from the flames and allow it to cool down while I grab another clay bowl and divvy up a portion for her before handing it over.

"Oh, thanks." Her gaze has not left me once, her proud smile twisting into pursed lips. The silence between us feels loud. She brings the bowl to her mouth, still eyeing me quizzically as if I am a puzzle she is yet to solve, and slurps at the stew. My right eye twitches at the obnoxious sound, but it is soon forgotten as she lets out a moan, closing her eyes, and taking another mouthful.

"Fates," I curse, my cock instantly springing back to attention. I am going to have to take matters into my own hands once she is asleep to satisfy this driving need the mate bond is forcing upon us. Perhaps if I tend to my own needs, my body will not be so quick to respond so willingly.

"This is the best thing I've ever tasted." She smiles at me, wiping her mouth on her arm. "It's been so long since I've had a home-cooked meal—well, mountain-cooked, I suppose." She chuckles to herself. I preen at her compliment. It is my duty to care for my mate, feed them, and ensure they are well cared for. Her compliment of the meal I have cooked for her makes that primal beast inside me glow with pride. Perhaps, I shall give her something for her efforts after all.

"Asterion."

"What?" That infuriating eyebrow cocks at me as she takes another mouthful of stew.

"My name. It is Asterion."

"Oh." I am almost certain I hear her mutter 'more like Ass-terion' into her bowl. I huff, already regretting my decision to tell her.

The silence between us is only broken by the spitting of the twin fires, the branches popping and hissing as the flames devour them. We eat side by side, looking out across the island as the sun finally disappears and is replaced with a thousand twinkling stars.

"Katie," she says, handing me her empty bowl. "Thanks for the food."

I nod, setting it aside as she curls up on her side by the fire with her back to me and drifts off to sleep. I sit there a little longer, watching the rise and fall of her ribs with every steady breath she takes. *Katie.* That is the name of my mate.

I clean up our bowls and put them away, the anticipation of finally having some alone time making me rush. I quickly lay out the fur I am to sleep upon and feel a pit of guilt at seeing her lying on the hard ground with nothing to soften it. A good mate would offer his fur up, but all the guilt in the world would not see me do that. I think back to this morning, waking up with her pressed against me. She was all hard angles, albeit warm. Her hand had mistakenly grabbed my cock, the traitorous thing instantly standing to attention with her against me.

The longer we ignore the mate bond, the more pressing the need to bed my mate becomes. If I do not take matters into my own hands soon, I will come merely from looking at her. It is already bad enough that her scent drives me mad whenever she is close, transforming me into nothing more than a wild beast eager to rut into anything to relieve the pressure. The fact that she is a vicious creature does nothing to deter my body, despite my mind being made up.

I glance toward her again, ensuring she is asleep before sneaking as far away as the rope will let me. I am not foolish enough to untie it lest it is all a ruse, but I will have to be quiet, and quick, though I fear the latter will not be a problem. My balls ache for release, my loincloth already tented. I give the knot at the base of my cock a firm squeeze, letting out a small groan. I turn my back toward our makeshift camp and spit into my hand, gripping my cock tight as I begin to stroke myself.

I try not to think of the little violet-haired viper that sleeps curled up mere feet away. I try not to think about the cloying scent of strawberries seeping from her pores that has tortured me thus far, nor how she grabbed my hand when I inspected her wounds and how soft they felt against my skin. I stroke faster, harder, biting down on my other arm to keep from making too much noise and waking her. I do not think about the way she smiled at me when we got the flint to light her fire; the first look of proper happiness she had shown, and I definitely do not think about her looking at me like that again, or what it would be like to elicit the same response as when she tasted the stew I made. Of how those plump lips would look parted around other things.

I stifle a groan as I paint the rocks with my seed, my knot inflating to almost painful levels with nothing to lock itself into. I grip it tight, hips stuttering slightly into my hand a couple more times, ensuring I am completely empty.

I let out a sigh, looking at my spend, wasted on the mountain rocks and not where it should be. Inside my mate. I shake my head, trying to clear it of the sleepy haze that comes after I have spent myself. Not her, though. It cannot be her. I grimace and turn back to our camp. Color drains from my face when I realize that Katie is no longer sleeping, the spot where she was resting now empty. Embarrassment flares hot on my face, knowing I must have woken her up. Perhaps I was too loud. I do not know what she heard or saw, nor how much.

I approach the fur and clear my throat. "Katie?" I call.

Perhaps she needed to relieve her bladder, though she could not have gone far with the rope binding us together. I give it a little tug, hopeful that a snarky remark will bite back from around the bend in the path. I am met with no resistance. Pulling again, the end of the rope comes into view, frayed and not attached to a little violet-haired viper.

12

KATIE

What a fool Asterion is to be so easily tricked. I hadn't thought my plan would work as well as it did. Some nice words and a couple of smiles to distract him, and he didn't even think of checking if I was really asleep. I grin to myself at my sheer dumb luck as I listen to him pottering around the campfire, the dishes clattering as he tidies up. Silence, then some rustling as I assume he readies his fur for sleep. Ever so slightly, I wiggle the knife out from my pocket, careful not to move too much and give myself away.

I frown, hearing his footsteps move away, the rope jiggling with each step, and it takes all of me not to look over at him. Why is he not sleeping? What is he doing? It occurs to me that maybe he's changed his mind and has just left me up here to rot, but then I realize I'm lying in the way of the path down the mountain. Maybe he's gone to fetch the Drakons instead, tired of carrying me already. Ice chills my veins. There is no better time than the present, then.

I am careful to muffle the snick as I unfold the pocketknife. A groan rings out, and I freeze like a deer in headlights, my body coiled and tense, ready to explode to my feet if he so much as breathes in my direction. When silence follows, I let my body relax. He's probably gone to take a piss. Taking the blade to the rope, I begin to saw. The rope, though roughly made, is thick and strong, and it takes me some time to cut through the first bunch of fibers. Wet slapping sounds echo out, and I still, straining my ears to figure out what the hell Asterion could be doing over there. There's a muffled moan, and my mouth pops open. Is he—

Heat crawls up my neck, making my face flush as I pause to listen to him stroke his cock. Wetness pools between my legs as my body begins to tingle. I catch myself panting in time with the slick slapping of his hand on his cock. I clench my thighs together, shaking myself out of whatever horny sex magic has overcome me. I saw faster, cutting my way through each strand of rope in what feels like a painstaking amount of time.

Finally, the last section splits apart, separating me from Asterion. I breathe a sigh of relief and quietly get to my feet, throwing a glance over my shoulder at the hulking form standing with his back to me, though not far enough away for my liking. For a moment, I am transfixed, watching the muscles along his back tense and ripple with each of his strokes. A shiver wracks my body, desire pooling low in my belly. I tell myself it's a lie, a falsehood, the mate bond or whatever. I am not attracted to the Minotaur, and I am certainly not interested at all in what he might be packing under that loincloth of his. Though I have gained some ideas over our short time together.

I trail the rope around the bend with me as I tiptoe away from the campsite, a small attempt to delay the chase I know is inevitable. Just let me get as far away as I possibly can first. A chance, no matter how small, is still a chance, and I'll take every opportunity I can get to live life on my terms. I didn't shoot my abuser and go on the run from corrupt law enforcement just to be handed over to a couple of monsters who may or may not eat me.

I drop the rope, and without looking back, I take off on a light jog back down the mountain path. The light from the campfire disappears quickly around the bend. The stars in the night sky do little to illuminate the path before me, but I cannot afford to slow down. The darkness makes it treacherous, but it'll be mere moments before he realizes I've run away again, and he'll be after me.

I stumble, a rock catching my boot, causing my ankle to twist painfully. I hiss as I go down on one knee, biting my tongue to not yell out. Tears spring to my eyes, partly because of the pain and partly because I know this will slow me down more. Whimpering, I stand, testing the weight on my sprained ankle. Pain shoots up my leg, but I'm still able to walk on it. No longer able to jog, I limp slowly down the mountain.

My breaths come in pants as sweat trickles down my back. The night has a chill, but I barely feel it as I attempt to navigate any more loose rocks in my path. I'm surprised I haven't been caught yet. Surely Asterion has noticed I'm missing by now, but perhaps he hasn't. He could very well still be masturbating for all I know. I lack all knowledge of Minotaur biology; maybe it takes them a long time to come. The memory of his grunts and groans, and the way his arm moved with each stroke, flares back to life with startling clarity. The ache between my legs has only slightly abated due to the distraction my sore ankle has provided.

I throw my head back and look at the sky, my pace slowing before I decide I need a rest and to check my ankle again. Sitting with my back against the rocky wall, I struggle to remove my boot, giving my foot a little wriggle when it's free. My ankle is swollen and sore to the touch. I need to stay off it; however, that's not an option. I huff and rest my head against the rock. Weariness seeps deep into my bones as I look out over the land before it meets the water, the moon reflecting off the sea in the distance.

Not everyone would think they were lucky to find themselves stranded in the middle of who knows where, but not everyone is me. If I didn't have Asterion on my ass, this would be as good as a holiday. Almost. Once I shake him, I'll be free. Freer than I've been in a long time. Stars blink in and out in the sea of black above me. Now that I've stopped moving, the ache between my legs grows more persistent, and my walls pulse as if trying to grip something. Sighing, I decide I may as well stop here for the rest of the night. I overestimated how much I'd be able to see, and now, with my ankle, I may as well just wait for Asterion to catch me.

The discomfort from my ankle and the persistent throbbing between my legs make it impossible to relax and get some sleep. I grow frustrated that Asterion hasn't caught up to me yet. What could he possibly be doing that takes so long? Maybe he's decided that gone is gone, and it doesn't really matter if he doesn't return me to the Drakons so long as I'm not bothering him.

I let out an exasperated cry. If I could just get some relief, I might be able to sleep, or think, or both. I can't do anything about my ankle right now, but I can solve one problem. I undo the button and zipper on my jeans, slipping my hands beneath the waistband. My underwear is already soaked from the brief glimpse I had of Asterion, and I move them to the side. My clit is already so sensitive when I tentatively brush the tips of my fingers against it. I let out a shaky breath, closing my eyes and applying pressure, rolling the bud beneath my fingers. My hips buck, a soft moan escaping me. It's been a long time since I've found pleasure in being touched, Greg all but destroying that part of me, but here in this moment, my body is perched on the precipice. One rightly timed stroke and I know I'll fall over the edge of my climax.

My mind wanders back to Asterion stroking himself, tenting his loincloth, the silken skin of his cock in my hand. I dip a finger inside of me. I'm so wet that it's not enough. Adding another finger, I pump them in and out while my other hand applies pressure back on my clit. I let out a soft moan as I pump and swirl simultaneously, my hips rocking with the motion. I whimper. I'm so close. I think about Asterion at my back with his nose in the crook of my neck, at my front with his body pressed in close, being bracketed by his arms and thighs as he moves my hands for me. I gasp as the waves of an orgasm roll over me, my walls fluttering and tightening around my fingers.

"What do we have here, little viper?"

My gasp chokes off into a scream as I scramble to my feet, stumbling when I put weight on my swollen ankle and fall forward. Asterion takes two steps toward me, catching me in his arms and walking me backwards until my back is pressed against the rocky wall. We stare at each other, his nostrils flaring as I grab onto his biceps. My mouth is agape at being busted with my hands down my pants, when he tilts his snout and inhales deeply. Horror floods me as I realize what it is he can smell, and I snatch my hands away from him, attempting to balance on one foot. With a growl, he snatches my hands back, holding me firm around the wrists as he brings one hand up and places my fingers inside his mouth. I can't think of a single thing to say as his warm, rough tongue sucks any traces of myself off my fingers. His tongue stills, pupils blown wide as I gently pull them out of his mouth and his eyes flutter shut.

"*Exactly* how I thought you would taste." He huffs before bending down and throwing me over his shoulder.

13

ASTERION

MINE.

This changes everything, and yet it changes nothing. She is mine. Her scent is mine alone. I have crossed a line I can never uncross. Now that I have tasted *her*, it will be almost impossible for me to leave her, and yet I must. The Drakons must be taught a lesson. They cannot just leave women in my labyrinth for their own amusement. I am not their puppet, and I refuse to play their games. But this woman slung over my shoulder, and her Fates-forsaken scent might send me into oblivion. Her scent that I will never be able to get out of my mind, my nostrils, nor off my tongue. I fear that everything may taste like ash after having tasted something so sweet as her. Even now, her undoubtedly wet, cloying cunt is a hairs-breadth from my nose, and if I had no sense at all, I would throw her down and rut into her right here. Fortunately, I do still have some

91

semblance of self-control, though I have no doubt it would only take something minor to crush it into dust.

The soft, warm glow of two dying fires barely illuminates our camp.

"Sit," I command, sliding her off my shoulder, carefully this time, so as not to hurt her injured ankle any further. There are things I need to do before I can settle down for what remains of the night, and I do not trust this tricky little viper one bit. "Stay."

"Woof." She barks at me, saluting me with two fingers striking off her forehead. My gaze flicks to the two fingers I had in my mouth only moments ago, before she realizes the attention she has drawn to them. Saliva pools on my tongue at the thought of doing it again. As if she can read my mind, her face flushes as she tucks her hands under her thighs. If only hiding them from sight would erase the loss of self-control from our memories.

I eye her distrustfully, expecting her to move as soon as I turn my back on her, before collecting a few more twigs for the fire and stoking the dying embers back to blazing. I turn back to her, kneel on the furs, and place her injured ankle on my lap. She frowns to herself, and I wonder what is going on inside that wicked little head of hers. She hisses as I test the limitations of it by moving it side to side. Her ankle is red and swollen, but it could be worse.

"This will need to be rested, unless you plan on another escape attempt before the morning?" I place her foot back on the fur and she tucks it beneath her with a sigh.

"Probably not much point is there? You'll only catch me again."

"You did not make it very far," I say pointedly.

Her face turns an even deeper shade of pink. "I wouldn't have had the opportunity if you weren't otherwise occupied," she snaps back.

"And you thought to return the favor? So... generous of you." I lean forward with a smirk. I no longer have to guess if she also saw me taking matters into my own hands.

My proximity has her leaning away from me, falling to rest on her hands to keep herself propped up. We are nose to nose when she scoffs, and I cock my eyebrow at her in question, my hand tracing her upper thigh through her pants.

"I was not thinking of you," she spits, but the way sweet strawberries waft from her flushed skin gives her lie away.

"Are you sure, little viper?" I croon. "I was thinking of you."

Her nostrils flare as her breathing catches. Growling, her hand goes for the little knife she has been keeping hidden in her pocket. The sharp little blade she has made sure I have become well acquainted with in the short amount of time we have spent together.

"Uh, uh, uh." I wiggle a finger in front of her, causing her to pause. "Looking for this?" I flip the knife in my hand, the one that I slipped from her pocket while she was too busy blushing at me. She scowls, a slight wrinkle appearing between her eyes as she pushes me back, lunging for it.

I jump to my feet, tucking it in the waist of my loincloth. "If you want it, you will have to come and get it." I smirk at her.

"Argh!" she shrieks, fists curled at her sides. "You are an asshole! A menace! A—!"

"A beast?"

"Yes!" She crosses her arms and legs at the end of her tantrum.

"Do not forget it," I growl. I am all those things and more. "If you are done, I have had a long night catching little vipers in the dark, and I would like to get some sleep before the sun rises."

I settle back down on the fur, picking her up and moving her over so I have room.

"Hey! What are you doing?"

"Sleeping." I lay down on my side, pulling her down with me before trapping her inside my arms. Not optimal sleeping conditions, but I will not have her sneaking away and hurting herself again.

"Let me go!"

"No."

She is tucked in against me, her back planted against my chest, and she attempts to wriggle free from my grip. I scrunch my eyes shut and huff as her behind presses against my cock. The Fates have cursed me. What is it about this little viper that has her so insistent on running away? Already, I can feel my cock hardening again. We do not need a repeat of earlier. Taking matters into my own hands has only made the mate bond angry and unsatisfied. It was not enough. It will not ever be enough until my cock is seated inside her dripping cunt, and the longer we ignore the bond, the worse it will get for us both.

"I suggest you stop moving," I mutter into her hair, causing her to still with a deep sigh. "And keep those hands to yourself."

She grumbles, wriggling once more before finally settling with another exasperated sigh. I told her I needed to sleep, but truth be told, I think it will be nearly impossible. The image of her head tilted back against the rock, lips slightly parted as she writhed beneath her fingers, is seared in my brain. Every time I close my eyes, it is all I can see. It felt indecent to stand there and witness her most private moment, yet I have never seen such a beautiful sight as the one of her coming undone with pleasure. A stark contrast to the girl with the biting tongue and the sharp words she is always quick to use.

Katie finally gives in to sleep; her breathing comes soft and slow with a little huff at the end of each breath. It should not be endearing. Nothing about her should be, but I smother a small smile anyway. If the circumstances were different, I would gladly welcome a mate into my furs. I would love nothing more than to share soft moments curled up together beneath the stars, but this is all wrong. She is not here by choice. They never are. What if I had done exactly what was expected of me? What if I had killed her? The Drakons were cruel to play such a trick. The Fates even crueler for binding us together as mates. The hunter and his prey.

14

KATIE

"Is this really necessary?" I grumble from over Asterion's shoulder. All my wounds are much better. The swelling in my ankle has gone down, and the bandage soaked in the healing spring water has returned the raw skin around my waist to pale and unmarked. I do not need to be thrown over his shoulder like I'm a sack of potatoes.

"Yes." A Minotaur of many words.

I have come to the conclusion that Asterion doesn't like to talk all that much, and usually that would suit me just fine. After a few months on the streets, I have also become quite comfortable with the silence that comes with being on your own more often than not. Compared to Greg yelling, I much prefer it. But there's just something about Asterion that makes me want to poke and prod and push at those boundaries. A feeling I never had with Greg.

Poking Greg was like poking a bear. You'd rather the bear. Poking Asterion is... fun.

Despite his insistence on taking me to the Drakons, he hasn't tried to eat me, and he's tended to my wounds even though I've stabbed him twice. He's even fed me. If that's all it takes for me to decide he's a safe space, the bar really is low. But do I trust him? That remains to be seen. It's clear he doesn't trust me—and for good reason. Even now, as we get closer to the Drakons, I'm still looking for opportunities to escape. Being thrown over Asterion's shoulder is making that far harder to achieve.

I huff another sigh. Asterion's shoulder is probably going to leave a bruise on my stomach with all the jostling as he carries me up the mountain, and it'll have been a waste of the water to heal the rope burn. He's such a brute.

"What's your deal with the Drakons anyway?" I ask.

"I would never make a deal with the Drakons."

I roll my eyes at how he takes everything so literally. "I mean, what is your issue?"

There's silence for a beat or two, and I don't think he's going to answer.

"The Drakons can be cruel. They have played this trick on me many times before—a long time ago. Before we were sequestered to Aeolia."

The Drakons sound like dicks, and yet Asterion is going to give me to them. Does he not see how that makes him just like them?

"What trick?"

"I do not wish to speak of it."

The end. Kapeesh.

I sigh again. "Are we there yet?"

"No."

I wait a few minutes. "What about now?"

"No."

I let the silence drag on until he thinks I'm done.

"Now?" I purse my lips, trying my hardest not to laugh.

He growls, his grip tightening around my thighs, causing arousal to flare to life at my core. We both groan simultaneously, and he stops immediately, sliding me to stand on my own two feet in front of him.

He bends so we're face to face. "I have been itching to put my hand across your backside until you are dripping and needy and begging me for more. Unless that is something you want, I suggest you be quiet."

I swallow thickly. "Quiet, it is," I squeak. I've never thought about being smacked as a form of pleasure. The idea of someone raising their hand at me again has my skin breaking out in a sweat. Very conflicting feelings swirl around my brain. I shouldn't want him to do what he's said, so why does the way he said it have me rubbing my thighs together in anticipation?

"You will walk now. I cannot stand the smell of you."

I scoff, slightly offended. I haven't showered in three days. Of course I stink.

"You don't smell any better," I jab, taking a discreet sniff in Asterion's vicinity, hoping to find the truth to my insult, except all he smells like is the wood fire from last night.

He cocks an eye at me like he knows exactly that before spinning me around and giving me a small shove forward.

"You will walk in front, little viper. I would not want you to slip away from me again when we are so close."

"So, we are close?" I smirk over my shoulder at him, and he scowls back.

"You know, I don't see what the difference is in handing me over to the Drakons and just letting me be on my merry way. Either option has you free of me."

"I do not know how they did it, but they brought you here. It is their responsibility to return you to where you came from."

"Two things." I hold up two fingers over my shoulder as we continue up the mountain. "I don't think the Drakons brought me here, and I don't want to go back to where I came from."

"What do you mean you do not think the Drakons brought you here?"

"Well, I woke up on the beach. The Drakons were already there, yes. But so was this shipping container, and it looked like it had been through a paper shredder or something. And also, it's all still a bit hazy, but I'm pretty sure it was some of my ex's goons that kidnapped me. One of their names was Lachesis, which is kind of strange if you ask me, and I'm pretty sure they drugged me, considering how awful I felt when I woke up."

I shiver at the hazy memory of a gummy smile and a horrible raspy cackle.

"I do not understand. You saw Lachesis? You were not dumped in my labyrinth by the Drakons?"

"Oh no, I wandered in there myself looking for water and got lost."

He grabs my shoulder, turning me to face him. "The Drakons did not put you in my labyrinth."

"I just said that."

It's as if he needs to repeat it for it to make sense to him. I wasn't even sure what I was seeing was real at the time.

"Lachesis is one of the Fates. This has been their doing. Why did you not say anything sooner?"

"You didn't ask. The Fates are real people?" *Who brought me here? Why?*

"Deities, not people." He groans, running a hand over his face. Then, without a word, he turns around and walks back down the path, leaving me standing there, halfway up a fucking mountain with my mouth hanging open.

"HEY! Now you're leaving me? What about the Drakons?" I yell after him, but he's already vanished from my sight.

"Fuck."

What are my options? Stay here, where the Drakons will likely stumble across my path, since there's only one of them. Stay here, and the Drakons don't stumble across my path, because who knows how often they travel it. I might die of exposure before then. Or I can follow after Asterion. At least until we get back down to the bottom of the mountain, and then I'll do... something. Anything. As long as it's not with him.

"Fucking fuck." I kick the rocky wall and then set off back down the mountain after Asterion, grumbling the entire way.

Asterion's legs eat up the distance down the mountain much quicker than we managed on the way up. Probably because he isn't carrying me or having me slow him down. I don't catch sight of him again until night begins to fall, and I hate to say that it's only because he stopped to make camp for the night.

Goose pimples prick my skin as a cool wind whips at my hair, and I attempt to rub some warmth back into my exposed arms. The change in temperature happens so suddenly that I look out expecting to see storm clouds brewing on the horizon, yet there is nothing but clear candy floss-colored skies as the sun begins its descent on another day up this fucking mountain.

Seeing the orange glow of the campfire throw shadows across the side of the mountain has me sighing in relief. I pick up my pace, eager to warm myself by it. Asterion is cooking something in his clay pot that smells divine as I tentatively approach. What if he doesn't let me stay? That's what I wanted originally, right? Except now, we're both heading in the same direction. It only makes sense to stick together until we reach the bottom. Plus, he has food.

My stomach growls right on cue, and Asterion glances my way at the sound.

"Um, hi." I do a small finger wave. He turns back to his cooking without saying a word. "Do you mind if I stay with you until we get back down the mountain?"

"There is no we." He doesn't look up from his pot, giving it a little stir.

"No, right. I know. I'll be out of your hair as soon as we're at the bottom. I promise."

He doesn't acknowledge me, and I take it as a good sign because he's not shooing me away either. I park myself right next to the fire. The breeze picks up again, making the flames flicker wildly and causing me to shiver. I look around at the sky that continues to darken, still expecting it to pour down with rain any moment now, but again, there's nothing.

Asterion hands me a small bowl of broth, and I slurp it down greedily, groaning as I'm warmed up from the inside out. I don't know how something so simply made can taste so heavenly. Maybe I've just had too many cold cans of spaghetti, or maybe Asterion is some kind of Minotaur wizard in the kitchen.

"Are you magic?" I break the silence.

"No."

I nod, expecting nothing less than his typical one-word answer.

"Are you?"

Shocked, I snort. "No."

"Why do you ask me such a thing?"

"This broth is so good. I just wouldn't be surprised if you magicked it into existence at this point." If I'm not mistaken, I see the hint of pink tinge his cheeks beneath his fur. I guess he doesn't get many compliments.

"Can you cook?"

I look over at him, surprised that he's asking me questions. Are we having an actual conversation?

"I can. I just haven't had much need to lately."

I expect him to pry, or maybe I'm just so used to the nosiness of people, but he takes my answer as it is, nodding in silence. Should I tell him I was on the run? Living on the streets? That I shot my ex? Would he care? Would he be horrified to know I almost murdered a man? One who would've deserved it, sure, but people still tend to frown upon almost killing others. I don't know what I'd say if he asked. I don't know why I care.

15

ASTERION

We sit in companionable silence, watching the flames dance as the sun finally disappears. There is a chill to the air that I have not felt before, even for being so high on the mountain, where it is usually cooler than underground in my labyrinth.

I should not have walked off and left Katie all alone. The Drakons could have stumbled upon her, and I do not know what they might have done. I was so angry at myself for not having thought to ask her anything. *Anything at all.* One simple question would have solved the problem, and we would not have spent three days playing cat and mouse up this Fates-forsaken mountain for no damned reason.

Though I suppose it has not all been terrible. The vision of Katie reaching climax is not one I will soon forget, and if she had not followed me back, I may have taken my cock in hand once more to relieve some of the tension that rides my spine. The mate bond is an angry, hungry beast, and already, three days is too long for us not to have sealed our bond. I wonder if she feels it too. This constant gnawing at the enclosure that keeps my soul contained, knowing the other half of it is right there. Sitting by the fire. So close, I could reach out and touch her.

I glance over at her. The glow from the fire makes her skin luminescent. I am entranced by the reflection of the flames dancing in her dark brown eyes, eyes I never took enough notice of before, and I think perhaps she lied about not being magic, because for once, I cannot look away.

A fleck of something lands on her cheek, and before I can stop myself, I reach over to brush it off. I think it could be a piece of ash that might burn her, but it is cold instead, melting under my touch to leave a dewy smear over her cheek. Frowning, I look at my fingers, rubbing the wetness between them.

"What is it?" She brushes her fingers against the same spot on her cheek.

"Water."

"Oh, I knew it was going to rain!" She looks at the sky. "Huh. Still no storm clouds. Maybe it'll just be a sprinkle." She shivers as a breeze brushes against her skin. The temperature feels as if it has dropped even more so now that night has fallen.

"It does not rain here."

She jerks her head to stare at me. "What do you mean it doesn't rain?"

"Exactly that. When the Moirai shut us away on Aeolia, they made it so it was perpetually spring. The temperature is always moderate and sunny. No rain. No storms. No cold," I explain, longing in my voice.

"I'm sorry, I'm lost. What is the Moirai? What do you mean it's always spring? It's cold right now. You said you felt water." Katie's voice becomes more high-pitched as she speaks. Her strawberry scent sours, giving away her anxiety as she wrings her hands.

I sigh. "The Moirai are the Fates. They locked all the monsters away, here on Aeolia, as human technology advanced and put us at risk of either extinction or war. It was safer for us, and for humans. But we have paid the price for that safety. A millennium alone here, frozen in time. No aging, no dying, no change. It is the same every day. The seasons do not turn. The sun stays shining. We wake up, and we begin again."

I long for summer rains, of fall leaves coating the ground, and the chill winter air that has you seeking the warmth beside a hearth fire. I can barely remember what it was like.

"A millennium?" Katie stares at me as if I have grown two heads. "You've been here that long?" She shakes her head in disbelief. I would not believe it either if I had not lived it myself.

I hum. "This chill, it is unnatural. I think something may be wrong. With either the Fates or the barrier itself. Perhaps we should not stop for the evening."

The thought of being exposed out here while something strange is happening on the island has the hairs along my neck standing up. I do not like it one bit. I like it even less with Katie here. So small and fragile. So easily injured.

"The last time I went walking in the dark didn't turn out so well for me, remember?"

"I remember." I could not forget it even if I tried.

"Please, no more throwing me over your shoulder," Katie pleads.

She explains what a piggyback is, and I secure the pack around her back and crouch down so that she can climb atop mine. She slings her arms around my neck, her head resting on one of them so that our faces are side by side for a change, and her thighs straddle my waist from behind.

"Ugh, you have to hold me up." She squeaks, her legs slipping down my side so that she dangles from my neck.

Tentatively, I grab her behind the thighs and hike her back up, so she is sitting comfortably.

"Phew." She sighs, flicking her hair out of her eyes.

I kick dirt over the fire to put it out before making our way back down the mountain. I will walk all night if I must to make sure we cross as much ground as possible. Thankfully, Katie is light as a feather, and I must admit that if I had a Minotaur for a mate, it is likely I would not be able to do this. Though I also would not worry so much about their fragility either.

Soon after I begin walking, Katie's familiar soft snores sound next to my ear. I chuckle to myself. I am certain she could fall asleep almost anywhere. There is peace in the quiet darkness, with the stars above. The chill in the air intensifies as I continue down the mountain, until even I am starting to feel it seep beneath the thin layer of hair that coats my body.

Small white flakes begin to fall from the sky, yet they disappear as soon as they touch my body, melting away into nothingness. I keep a steady pace until there is enough of the powder falling that it no longer disappears, dusting the path and mountainside in a thin layer of white. It jogs my memory from long ago, and I know I have seen this before. Snow. It is snowing on the mountain. My heart kicks up a beat as my mind races through the handful of possibilities of what could be causing this. Not once has there ever been snow on Aeolia. So, why now?

I hesitate to wake Katie, but I am beginning to worry that she may fall ill to this strange cold if even I am beginning to feel its effects. There is still a long way to go down this mountain before we make it back to the caves, and we are exposed out here with no shelter—something I have never had to consider before, when the temperature is always moderate, and you never have to worry about being rained on, let alone stuck outside whilst it snows.

"Katie. Wake up." I jostle her a little on my back to wake her. She lets out a soft moan, and heat flushes my cheeks. I curse softly. Now is not the time for the mate bond to act up.

"Katie." I jostle her harder, giving her thighs a firm squeeze this time. She responds by grinding against my back with another soft moan. I want to know what she is dreaming about, my cock instantly standing to attention as her strawberry perfume fills the air.

"Fates save me," I grumble, looking skyward.

Deciding there is nothing else for me to do, I drop her.

"Aargh!" She lands on her behind on the now cold and wet path, the thin layer of snow causing it to soak into the back of her pants.

I quickly adjust myself as discreetly as I can in my loincloth before turning and helping her to her feet.

"I tried to wake you." I grab her hand, pulling her up.

She scoffs. "Sure, you di—"

Her mouth pops open, trailing off when she finally realizes her surroundings do not look the same as they did when we first started off. She spins, taking it all in.

"Is that—?"

"Snow," I confirm.

"What the hell?" She bends down, scooping up a handful of the white powder in her hand, letting it melt and drip between her fingers.

16

KATIE

The snow isn't quite thick enough along the path, turning it into a muddy, wet slush. The bottoms of Asterion's calves are splattered in it, matting the hair on his legs.

"I do not want you to get too cold. We still have quite a way to go."

He probably should've thought about that before dumping me on the ground. Already, I can feel the harsh bite of the cold through my clothes, especially now that the back of my jeans are soaked through.

He takes the pack from me, pulling out the fur and securing it around my body, tying it tight with the rope. I feel like a fluffy human sushi roll. He straps the pack back around me, the extra weight causing me to lose my balance. He grabs at the ropes, securing the fur and pulling me upright before I can tip all the way backwards.

"I hope you don't expect me to keep up with you like this. I can barely stand."

He snorts at me. "Of course not. I will carry you, but no more piggybacks."

I groan. "Fine. Let's get it over with." My arms are tucked inside the fur at my sides, so I'm completely at Asterion's mercy. It might be quicker if he just rolled me down the mountain instead.

"At least this way I will not have you grinding against me like a dog in heat."

I gasp. "I did not!" Heat rises up my cheeks.

"Yes, you did. Tell me, what were you dreaming about?"

Kill me.

He still has his fingers hooked around the rope to stop me from falling over, but it doesn't stop me from attempting to waddle toward the edge. He tugs me back to him, smashing me into his body. If it wasn't for the fur, I'd be face deep in his chest. His nipple rings wink at me in the moonlight.

"Where do you think you are going?"

I refuse to make eye contact, looking everywhere except at his face. I can't tell him that I was having a very good dream with him as the main attraction.

"Oh, I was just going to throw myself over the edge."

He cocks his head at me, bending down so that we're face to face, and I have no other choice but to look at him.

"Little viper." His rumbling voice sends tingles down my spine. "I have borne witness to you finger fucking yourself to climax. What is a little dry humping between friends?"

My mouth dries up looking into his rich golden-brown eyes.

"Are we friends now?" I can barely whisper it.

"You tell me."

For once, I am speechless, left standing there with my mouth opening and closing like a fish out of water. Is it hot out here, or is it just me? Am I overheating? I don't think I even need the fur anymore. I am a hot, sticky mess. Between my legs specifically. I am filled with an awful, terrible *need*.

Asterion hums. "If I had known the fur would smother your scent, I would have done this sooner."

In one swoop, he picks me up and throws me over his shoulder, and I finally come to my senses with a screech.

"Warn a girl, would you?" I'd smack him, but I can't. "And I know I smell, okay? That's what happens when you haven't washed in days."

"You think you smell bad?" Asterion continues down the mountain, at a much slower pace this time. Flurries of snow fall from the sky, making visibility almost impossible.

"Well, yeah, you've only said so a hundred times." I blow my bangs out of my eyes as I'm jostled around on Asterion's shoulder while he walks.

"The problem is not that you smell bad. It is that you smell good enough to eat."

Blood drains from my face. Has he been fighting the urge to eat me this entire time, and I've been teasing and testing boundaries, thinking it's all in good fun? I suddenly think about the dried meat he has been sharing with me, and I think I might be sick. What if it was... human?

"Oh no."

I have no hands to stop it. The sloshing of my stomach with every step Asterion takes, combined with dangling over his shoulder, has dinner coming back up my throat before I can do anything about it. I retch. Chunks of undigested meat and vegetables splatter across the mud, burning my nose on the way out.

"Katie!" Asterion gasps, sliding me back to my feet. I stumble away from him, unbalanced.

The coating of snow has gradually gotten thicker until the path has become less brown sludge and more sparkling white, only tainted by Asterion's footsteps.

"Did I—Did you—?" I struggle to get the words out. Just the thought of them makes my stomach turn again.

"What is it?" Asterion looks stricken as panic overtakes me.

"Did—Did you feed me human?" I'm so horrified. If I had my pocketknife, I'd probably have it pointed at his chest right now. I can feel my body tremor inside the fur. I so desperately want him to tell me it's not true.

"What are you talking about?" He frowns, stepping toward me.

I take another step back. "The meat. The dried meat! Is it... human?" Pain stabs at my chest like a knife through my sternum.

Breathing becomes harder to do until I'm buckled over, gasping through a panic attack.

Asterion takes another step toward me, arms out like he's placating a wild animal.

I shake my head to tell him not to come any closer as I struggle to breathe. Tears prick the corners of my eyes. My feet shuffle backwards away from him, the closer he gets, until the ground drops out from beneath my heels.

"Of course it is—"

I take a deep breath, my stomach in my throat as I tip over the edge, and I scream.

17

ASTERION

"Not."

One moment, Katie is standing right in front of me, asking me absurd questions about dried meat while in the throes of a panic attack, and the next moment, she is gone, her scream piercing the silence.

The moment repeats in my mind in slow-motion as I jump over the edge after her. The look of sheer panic in her eyes as she tipped backwards, her arms bundled up inside the fur so she could not even catch herself, is not a memory I will soon forget.

Snow coats the mountainside in a sea of white, obscuring jagged rocks and spindly shrubs beneath. It also makes spotting Katie nearly impossible as the fur she is wrapped in blends in with the surroundings. I slip and slide down the side of the mountain. Drifts of snow shift beneath me until I tumble, rolling some of the distance, before I find my feet once more. I catch a slice to the ribs at some point, but I do not feel it. The blood thumping in my ears drowns out all else. I have tunnel vision for Katie only, my gaze constantly zigzagging across the terrain, looking for anything that might give away her location.

"Katie!" I yell, my voice echoing out in the night.

Fear creeps its way into my chest, crushing my heart in its grip. I must not panic. I will find her. I rub at my sternum, at the steady ache that has settled there, and I tell myself that it is a good sign. The mate bond would cause me undeniable pain if the fall had been fatal. But I also know that she has been injured enough for me to feel it through the bond.

"Katie!"

All I want is to hear her snarky voice call out to me in return, but instead, the mountain behind me rumbles with a deafening roar, snow cascading down from high above in an avalanche. I curse, the snow chasing me toward the base. It takes me out at the knees until I am partly riding it. I have no choice but to let it drag me along, fighting to keep from being sucked beneath the surface.

"Katie." My voice cracks. I cannot see her anywhere, and then I cannot see anything at all, losing the battle to keep myself adrift. Snow tumbles over my head, turning white to black, pushing me along, and tossing me beneath icy cold waves. I collide with something solid, taking the wind out of my lungs. I feel like I am drowning.

18

Asterion

I gasp for air, breaking through the surface of the snow. Dawn is breaking, the sky lightening to a shade of gray as the evening fades. My temple throbs, my hand coming away sticky with blood. I must have been knocked unconscious at some point.

Birds twitter a sweet song nearby as if I have not just endured a nightmare. I claw my way out of the bitter cold grave with a feral roar. Ears ringing and vision spotty, I stumble to my feet, swaying on the spot before collapsing to my knees as the snow continues to shift with the after-effects of the avalanche.

"Katie!" My voice is hoarse, my throat raw. "KATIE!" I scream for her, breaking on a sob. She cannot be dead. I would know. *I would know.*

A choking, gasping cough sounds out from somewhere to my left. Heart racing, I scramble in that direction. I am slowed down by the snow, tripping and sinking in sections that come up to my waist. My fingers are red with cold as I pull myself back out on my hands and stomach. Strands of purple stain the white landscape. I collapse to my knees at the spot, chest heaving from exertion, and dig. I manage to free her face first, not far from beneath the surface. There's a gash on her cheek that has coagulated, a thin line of red that stands out against the ghostly gray of her skin. Her lips and eyelids are tinted purple. She coughs again on a rasping inhale.

I dig faster, like a beast possessed. There is roaring in my ears as my blood thunders in my veins. A thin sheen of sweat coats my body as the gray of twilight becomes pastel purple, then pink. I do not know how long it takes me, only that I do not stop until she is free. I heave big gasping breaths, my fingers raw and bloody by the end.

By some miracle, she is still bound in the fur. I unwrap her gently, revealing all her limbs tucked safely inside. The thickness of it has done the bulk of protecting her frail body. I choke back a sob of relief at not finding any serious wounds. I reluctantly shift her to check for any head injuries since it seems to have taken the brunt of the damage with the cut across her cheek. Color drains from my face as I reveal a pool of blood beneath her, the back of her hair matted and stained a dark red along with the snow. My hands tremor as I feel for the wound on the back of her skull, breath hitching as I trace an inch-long gash. This wound could be fatal given how much blood has been lost, and I worry that if I do not get her to the Pierian Spring soon, I might lose her.

Wasting no more time, I wrap the fur around her once more. She has been lucky that it stayed secure, helping to keep her as warm as possible, and I have a horrible feeling that if it had not, I would have found her much too late. As gently as I can, I cradle her in my arms, not daring to throw her over my shoulder this time. I grunt as my ribs throb. Now, as the adrenaline wears off, my own wounds begin to make themselves known.

The spring will heal us both. I just have to get us there.

With weary bones and cuts that sting with every movement that reopens them, I push through the snow. We fell quite a way down the mountain, not far from the base. Not far from home. The thought keeps me moving, one foot in front of the other. I do my best not to fall into any more pits, holding Katie high on my chest as one takes me by surprise with a grunt, sinking me to my thighs.

As the sun moves higher in the sky, the snow begins to melt, making the journey easier when solid ground reveals itself.

We pass through the meadow we camped in on the very first night. How she wound up in my arms that evening remains a mystery, though I suspect the mate bond had us naturally gravitate toward each other in our sleep. My body screams with each step closer to the cave entrance. So much so that I begin to pant with the pain that jars through my ribs, and I suspect I may have broken one. But I will not put Katie down for anything. I grit my teeth and balance across the rocky outcrops that break up the long grass. Katie's color has not returned; instead, perspiration beads across her forehead and upper lip. Her scent is all wrong, too. The tang of rotten strawberries seeps from her pores.

We are almost there.

The cave entrance comes into view, and I close my eyes with a sigh, apologizing to the Fates for having ever used their name in vain. Grunting, I close the distance, the dark enveloping us in its comforting embrace. *Home.* We are so close I can almost hear the tinkling of the water as it trickles into my bathing spring, fed from the Pierian Spring that sits directly beneath the mountain. I increase my pace, winding through the labyrinth, thankful to see its walls for a change, until at last, glow worms guide us to exactly where we need to be.

The warm steam rising from the spring casts an almost suffocating fog, the walls slick with moisture. Fresh fear coats the back of my throat, almost making me gag on it. What if I am too late? I carefully set Katie down at the edge and unwrap her from the fur. I step into the heated water myself, not bothering to undress, the water instantly seeking my wounds and weaving around my aching bones to heal any injuries it can find. Already, I notice the difference as the sting of a cut on my back is replaced with a soothing feeling.

I gently pick up Katie, sliding her into the water fully clothed until she is submerged, with only her face above the surface. Blood inks the water in floaty tendrils as it washes out of the strands of her hair. I watch her face intently, looking for any sign of change, the color returning to her cheeks, or the fluttering of eyelashes. Moments go by, and nothing happens. I growl in frustration. Perhaps more of her skin needs to be exposed, though it has not been needed before when I have faced greater injuries. But I do not know what else to do.

With great difficulty, I begin to strip her of her clothing, slapping the wet fabric on the stone floor. I leave her in the smaller strips of fabric that conceal the most intimate parts of her from roaming eyes—my roaming eyes. She is covered in a smattering of bruises from the fall, angry purple and black ones on her thighs, stomach, and back. I grimace. Now, without all the layers, I can see how truly scrawny she is. Not just small in stature, but showing signs of undernourishment, the outline of her ribs easily visible. I am surprised the breeze did not just pick her up and blow her off the mountain after all.

The mate bond flares to life, angry. But not for us to consummate the bond. Instead, I am urged to feed her, care for her, and bring her back to life. I feel sick with myself that I never noticed the extent of her fragility. Chalking it up to her just being a tiny human and not because she looks like she has never had enough to eat. Her comments about my simple broth and how she gulped it down like someone starved make more sense to me now. Because she was. *Is.*

I pound my fist into the water with a splash. "Come on!"

I urge the spring to work its magic like I can feel it doing to my own body. Frustration grows as Katie remains unconscious. We stay there for hours, soaking in the spring as our injuries slowly heal. I assume it must be nightfall when I finally feel as if I am fully healed. My ribs no longer scream at me with each movement, and the numerous cuts along my arms and legs have long since sealed themselves. Still, Katie does not wake.

We stay there all night, with her battered body cradled in my arms. Her bruises fade, and I trickle water along the cut on her cheek, wiping away the line of crusted blood that remains after the edges seal themselves back together. I wash the remainder of blood from her hair, detangling it with my fingers as I go, making sure the gash at the back of her skull is clean. It also seals itself shut when I am done, the skin magically stitching itself together, though this one will likely leave a scar. The pallor of her skin is the last thing to change, rosy hues rising to the surface, turning the sickening gray back to pale, cheeks and lips flushed healthy again. But still, she does not wake.

When I start to feel myself drift off, unable to keep my eyes open any longer, I concede. The spring has done all it can; now it is up to her to do the rest.

19

ASTERION

I carry her limp body back to my hut. The mate bond causes me physical pain to see her state and fuels a burning fire inside me. She should be taking better care of herself, and if she cannot do it, I will. I tuck her into my bed of furs, piling more on top to make sure the cold does not have a chance to creep back into her bones. I keep the fire burning so hot that heat shimmers in the air, and sweat is my constant companion. I pull up my chair to the edge of the bed, and I do not leave her side.

I wipe at her skin with a damp cloth, cleaning the slick of sweat from her forehead and brushing the hair from her eyes, reminding me of every time she swatted at the violet strands or huffed at them as we trekked up the mountain. I brew a clear broth and help her drink it, cradling her head in my arms and being so careful not to let her choke. I take a chunk of wood from my stockpile and find my place in my chair by her side, whittling away at it with a knife while I wait for her to wake.

⁂

I wake with a start.

She stirs in the night, tossing and turning, kicking off furs and screaming out in the dark.

"Shhh." I reach for her hand, taking it in mine.

Her screams turn to whimpers before she settles again.

⁂

I finish making a comb for her, gently brushing out the tangled and matted strands of hair while she sleeps. It is hours before I am satisfied it is free from knots. I manage to get her to take more broth. She sighs, and I am startled when she rolls over to reach for my hand in her sleep. I do not pull it away.

20

Katie

I wake to a golden light basking me in the coziest warmth, so much so that I bury myself deeper into the blankets, not wanting to open my eyes and face the day. I can't remember the last time I woke up feeling warm and cozy, and as well rested as I do. It takes a millisecond to realize something is all wrong. I open my eyes under the covers, faced with the dark, while I figure out what the hell is going on and where I am.

The last thing I remember is the freezing cold of the snow on the mountain.

The mountain I fell off.

I throw the furs back with a gasp, sitting up and rubbing my hands all over my body to check for injuries. I pause when I realize I'm stripped down to my underwear. Blood drains from my face as I stare at my exposed and unblemished skin. It's disconcerting to know I should feel like I fell off a mountain, if I wasn't dead, but only my scalp feels tender. My fingers trace over a new scar on the back of my head. The wound is healed, but still sensitive to touch. It's the only sign that it really did happen.

One moment, I was panicking, and then the ground beneath me disappeared. I took one step too far backwards, my heel catching on the edge of the cliff. Asterion's look of horror as he disappeared, until it was only the sky above, the mountain below, and the flurries of snow drifting down around me while I fell. I could feel my stomach lurch into my throat to cut off my scream, and then I made contact with the ground, or some semblance of a hard surface—the mountainside covered in snow. I must've hit my head then because there is nothing after that.

What the fuck happened?

I register the room I'm in—mud brick walls, a familiar-looking chair off to the side. Asterion's home. No sign of him, though. There's a pressing need in my bladder, so I test my shaky legs on the floor, slipping out of what I assume is Asterion's bed. My face flushes with heat. Where has he been sleeping if I've been here? My body feels weak, like I've been bedridden for a few days. My knees give out beneath me and I go down with a yelp. Thunderous footsteps sound from outside before Asterion appears in the doorway.

"You are awake."

There's no time for pleasantries. "Bathroom!"

My heart flutters rapidly in my chest to see him, and I can't differentiate if it's from fear or relief.

He rushes to me, helping me up from the floor in one swoop, so I'm cradled in his arms, before he takes me outside and around the back of his hut. He places me on an oversized stool with a circle cut out of the middle over a rather deep hole in the ground. It's a long drop. I don't know why I'm disappointed to not find a flushing toilet—or a door. After everything I've witnessed so far, it's clear modern amenities aren't easily come by here, but it's an improvement over going to the bathroom in the open air of the mountain. Though that view was better.

"Do you need help?" His offer is genuine, and I shake my head, unable to speak. The embarrassment of needing him to carry me out here is enough.

"I will be around the corner. Call for me if you need."

I'd rather fall down this hole than call for his help. I bite my lip, trying to wiggle my underwear down while also making sure that doesn't happen. I sigh from the sheer relief of emptying my bladder, the tension melting from my body.

When I'm finished, I give my legs a firm talking to. We're going to walk back. We're not going to call for Asterion to help. I use the wall of the hut as leverage, using it to support me as I shuffle back around the front. Asterion looks up from where he kneels before his vegetable garden, jumping up and rushing to my side.

"I said to call for me," he growls, picking me back up in his arms and taking me inside to set me back down in his bed of furs. I don't protest even though I know I should. I don't have the energy to argue. I'm already exhausted again, and sleep pulls me under as soon as my head hits the furs.

"Eat."

I groan, stretching out my limbs like a cat in a warm patch of sunlight, before opening my eyes. I come face to face with Asterion, and I don't miss the heated gaze he rakes down my body. I gulp, pulling the furs I must've kicked off at some point back over me. Asterion's home is sweltering, leaving me with the sticky feeling of dried sweat over my skin. I ignore the bowl he holds in front of my face.

"Where are my clothes?"

"Eat, and I will tell you."

I scowl at him. "I'm not eating that."

He grabs my chin. "You will eat it."

"I won't." I clench my teeth. He'll have to pry my mouth open with his fingers if he thinks I'm going to eat anything he cooks for me. I may have fallen off a mountain, but I haven't forgotten what it was we were arguing about.

He looks at me as if prying my mouth open is exactly what he's thinking about doing.

He frowns. "Why not?"

I pull my chin out of his grip, surprised he asked me instead of just arguing with me again.

"I'm not eating human meat! You might have tricked me before, but now I know, I won't eat it again!" Just the thought of it has my stomach turning. I don't know how I'm supposed to live with the guilt of this dirty little secret I'll have to carry with me forever now.

He sighs, running his hand over his face, and I notice he looks tired and worn.

"It is not human meat." He rolls his eyes, shaking his head.

"You said—" I go to argue.

"If you had not fallen off the side of the mountain, you would have heard me finish my sentence. It is *not* human." He growls impatiently and shoves the bowl in my hands. "If you are so insistent on your assumption, perhaps I should show you what I really want to eat." He leans in so I'm face to face with him, and my heart skips a beat. My lady parts tingle, and I swallow thickly.

I look down at the bowl, noticing it's just a clear broth. It's probably safe. My eyes flick back to his.

"You swear?"

"I swear."

Against my better judgment, I lift the bowl to my lips and take a mouthful. It's delicious as usual, even for a clear broth. I'm pretty sure he could make a lump of dirt taste good.

"That's it. Swallow it all for me." Asterion growls in approval.

I squeak, squeezing my thighs together. His words tingle down my spine, right to my core. He closes his eyes, inhaling deeply with a satisfied hum.

When I've finished, I hand the bowl back to him. "Thanks."

A weight is lifted from my shoulders if I'm to trust that he's telling the truth, though I really have no reason not to believe him.

"It's a good thing I didn't overreact then," I say sheepishly.

There's a loaded silence between us as he takes my bowl to wash it up.

"So, um, how long have I been out for?"

"Four days." He keeps his back turned to me.

"Four days! You've looked after me this entire time?"

I've clearly been well cared for. My clothes are missing, and I assume he took me to the spring to heal any injuries I must've had. But more noticeably, my hair has been brushed, and my skin is clean, albeit sweaty. His chest rumbles with a growl, and I'm confused as to why he's acting so weird. What does he care if I eat or if my hair is brushed? Why does he help me? It's a far cry from the snippy asshole who dumped me on the ground every time he needed to wake me up. Maybe he fell and hit his head, too.

"Why did you rescue me? Why have you looked after me? Why... any of it? You were so eager to get rid of me, it doesn't make any sense."

His head bows as he grips the edge of the counter, his back muscles taut.

"Because even as frustrating as you are, I could not bear to see you die. My heart ripped itself to shreds inside my chest in its effort to follow you over that edge."

"Y-you followed me?"

"I will always follow you." He turns to face me, a serious look on his face as he crosses his arms over his chest.

"Is that a threat?"

"It is a promise, little viper."

21

KATIE

I don't know how to feel, how to act, or any of it. He followed me over the edge of a fucking mountain. What insanity must someone possess for them to do that for a person they don't even like? My thoughts flit to Greg. Greg would do that, only to ensure I was really dead.

"Once I'm back to a hundred percent, I'll leave," I assure him, nodding to myself.

"Did you not just hear me?" He growls, stalking back over to where I sit on his furs. "I will follow you wherever you go. Even if you were to leave, we could not be far apart without it causing us both physical pain. If one of us were to die, it would feel as if one half of ourselves had been cut from our chests, the pain indescribable. Life would not feel worth living. I have seen it happen."

We're face to face, and my eyes flick between his, noting the sincerity of his statement. I scrunch my eyebrows together.

"But—you wanted me gone. That was the whole point of marching me up that mountain in the first place. Now you're saying you want me to stay?"

He rubs his hand down his face, taking a seat in his chair by the bed.

"I thought you were a trick played by the Drakons. They have done it before, though not since the barrier has been placed around Aeolia. I just thought... I do not know what I thought." He shakes his head. "You must know, people—women, young girls—were often left in my labyrinth as sacrifices, with the expectation that I would either fuck them or eat them, or both." He looks disgusted, and my stomach roils, still unsure if I can really believe him on the human meat front. I wait for him to continue.

"I did not eat anyone." He looks at me pointedly, like he knows exactly what I'm thinking.

"Instead, each one lived out their painfully short human lives here with me in peace. It is how I learned many of the skills I now have, since I was abandoned as a child with no one else to teach me. I was happy to have the companionship for a short time. When the barrier went up, no one else could be offered as a sacrifice. It was a blessing and a curse, as the last of the females died from old age or sickness, until it was just me here on my own once more."

I feel tears pool in my eyes for him, having lived such a sad and lonely life. I quickly wipe the wetness away with a sniff.

"So, I thought the Drakons had placed you in my labyrinth to either fuck or eat. My anger insisted I seek them out so they could take you back to wherever you came from and punish them for it, too. In my haste, I did not bother to listen to you. That was my mistake. We could have avoided," he waves his hand around the air at us, "all of this."

"That is—a lot." I whistle. "Just so you know, I have no intention of going back to where I came from, even if I could figure out how."

"I have gathered, since you took every opportunity to escape me on that mountain."

I can't help but smirk at him.

"But now, we are mates, and we are stuck together for eternity." He slaps his knee and gets back up to potter around in what I assume is his kitchen area.

Hang on a minute. "You can't just say that like it's nothing," I exclaim, flabbergasted. "What if I did want to go home? What then?"

"But you do not. So, tell me, why?"

Ah, shit. I grimace. Where do I start? What do I tell him? What do I not tell him?

"I'm kind of wanted." Good, get it all out in the open.

"By whom?" He growls, and I reflexively flinch back at the sudden aggression. If he notices, he does not mention it. "They cannot have you. You are my mate."

"Uh, the cops. Law enforcement," I clarify, not really knowing what terms he would know. The idea of the cops running into a giant Minotaur is amusing. I wouldn't mind seeing how well that'd go down.

"You are a criminal?" He snorts. "That is not surprising."

"Hey!"

He shrugs unapologetically. "What did you do?"

"I shot my ex." He looks at me blankly. "I used a weapon and hurt my mate?" I grimace at the choice of words. A mate Greg was not. But I'm unsure how else to explain it in a way he'd understand.

"You hurt a mate?" He frowns, looking out the window.

"Yes, but um, he hurt me first. It was self-defense." I wring my hands in my lap.

He hands me another bowl of clear broth, his brow cocked as if he knows I'm going to argue. I do the opposite and take it, grateful to have something to do with my hands. His other eyebrow goes up in surprise. I sip on the delicious broth in silence while he supervises, glad his line of questioning seems to be over with, but nervous that he hasn't said anything. What if he kicks me out? I was going to go anyway, but then he insisted I have to stay, and I don't know what I'm going to do anymore.

"Are you going to say anything?"

"He hurt you often?"

I stare into the bowl in my hands, my reflection looking back at me in the broth. The girl staring back at me is not just a victim, she's a survivor. I made it out, and not everyone does. I straighten my back.

"Often enough."

"Then he is no true mate. He deserves whatever you did to him and more." He retrieves something, walking over and dropping it in my lap. My pocketknife.

"I just told you how I hurt somebody, and now you're giving this back to me?"

"It is unfortunately not the first time I have heard such stories. Thank you for telling me yours. I understand why this knife is never far from your hand now. It would comfort me to know that you have it, if that is what you need to feel safe."

I'm stunned into silence, putting the bowl to the side to trace the small knife in my lap.

"I, uh, don't want you to treat me any differently now that you know. I'm not fragile. I won't break."

He huffs a laugh. "You are fragile. But I understand."

I grumble, but am otherwise satisfied that he's not going to walk around on eggshells with me. I'm still trying to figure out who I am and who I can be, and I like having someone around whom I can bully a little, that I can push boundaries with, and learn what I'm comfortable with and still feel safe.

"I will let you rest some more. I will be in the garden if you need me."

I nod, watching him go with a strange aching in my chest. Why do I kind of want him to stay?

22

ASTERION

Katie rests for a few more days, takes some short walks around the vegetable garden with my help, and eats. I make sure I am already preparing her next meal by the time she is finished with the current one. Fresh vegetables I have grown, cured meats I have hunted, and citrus fruits I have picked from the orchard above. The mate bond sings every time she lifts a piece of food to her mouth, the hollow planes of her face and body already showing signs of filling out.

"I'm going to the spring," she announces.

"Yes, you smell." If she did not suggest it, I was soon going to. I have been unable to drift far from her side since bringing her back to my home. The mate bond is a constant, thrumming energy beneath my skin since we have not consummated it. It is only sated enough for me to continue functioning when I am feeding her. I also need to bathe, but it is further than she has walked yet while building her strength, so I have waited for her to be ready. "I will carry you."

"You always say I smell," she argues. "I don't need your help, I can walk."

"It is not just a short lap of the garden. I will carry you." As if I would let her walk on her own.

She rolls her eyes. "Fine. But can you give me a piggyback again? I don't need to be thrown over your shoulder for old time's sake."

I gather up some things to take with us, and she adds her pile of clothes to be washed. I will be disappointed to see her covered up again, so used to her wandering around in her underclothing. Securing the bundle, I crouch down for her to climb atop my back, and I take hold of her thighs to stop her from slipping. My mind flashes back to her grinding on me that very fateful night, right before she fell off the mountainside. I take a deep breath, willing my cock to stay down. A hopeless endeavor when I have her very naked skin in my hands and against my back. Her cunt is a hairsbreadth from where my fingers sit against her thighs.

"Giddy up!" Her small hands have taken a horn in each, pulling me out of the haze.

I scowl. "If you are not careful, little viper, I will give you something else to ride if that is what you are so eager for."

The tension has been riding me almost daily now. The urge to mate continues to grow stronger the more she does, and I often have to sneak outside in the middle of the night to take my cock in hand to relieve the pressure aching in my balls. She sniggers in my ear like she knows exactly what she is doing. My back vibrates beneath her in a growl, cutting her giggles off with a soft exclamation. Two can play at this game, mate.

I carry her the short way to the spring where I first found her, humidity misting the air and raising the temperature. Glow worms across the ceiling provide us with enough light to see by. The little specks of light reflect in the wet-slicked walls, making it feel as if we have been transported to another realm.

I can almost feel Katie thrumming with the excitement and anticipation of feeling clean. She slips down my back and runs into the water as fast as she can without slipping, splashing warm water over the edge as she sinks beneath the surface and comes back up with a gleeful sigh.

I chuckle, rummaging through the things I brought to throw her some soap berries.

"We have soap!" She laughs, catching them and lathering them in her hands before soaping up the rest of her body.

I untie my loincloth, letting it drop to the floor. I will wash it after I have washed myself. Katie yelps, dropping the soap berries and covering her eyes as I enter the water.

"Why are you naked!" She spins so her back is to me.

"I also need to wash." The water feels decadent against my skin, and I dive beneath the surface to fetch the soap berries, coming back up in front of Katie.

"I am covered," I huff with a laugh. "You can open your eyes."

She peeks between two fingers before splashing me. "You could've warned me."

"It did not occur to me that you would not be accustomed to seeing nudity."

"I am accustomed, thank you very much. I was just shocked. If you don't care, then I don't care. I need to wash these anyway," she says haughtily and begins to unfasten her underclothing, stripping away both halves until she is all bare skin everywhere, though the spring shields everything below the water from view. She raises her eyebrows at me as if to say 'see?' and I roll my eyes and shake my head at her with a chuckle before soaping myself up.

We keep a short distance from each other as she takes her items of clothing, soaps them up, and washes them out before slapping them on the wet stone floor.

"We can hang them up to dry back at home," I tell her as I do the same to my own.

"Yeah, I just didn't think about what I was going to wear after this. I don't have anything else."

"I have an extra loincloth. I can wrap you in it if you like?"

She turns to face me, a pink flush creeping up her neck. "Oh, thanks. What will you wear?"

"I will air dry." I wiggle my eyebrows at her, and she splashes me again, grumbling.

She begins soaping up her hair and rinses it out, attempting to untangle it with her fingers, cursing as the knots refuse to budge.

"Come here." I grab the comb I made for her while she was unconscious from the bundle of things I brought with us and slide up behind her. Taking the strands of hair from her hands, I gently work the comb through the knots from the ends to her scalp, taking extra care at the sensitive spot where her head wound was.

"Why do you have a comb?" She tries to turn her head to look at me, and I move her back to facing forward.

"I made it for you."

"You made it—for me?" She attempts to turn again.

"Stay still. Yes, how do you think I managed to comb the knots out of your hair when you were unconscious?"

She's quiet as she shrugs. "I don't know. I've never had anyone take care of me like that. It never occurred to me that you would make something I needed."

I grunt, knowing the topic she is skirting around, her shoulders bunched up tight.

I manage to get her hair tangle-free and then take the soap berries and lather up her back, using firm strokes to work away at the knots that have made their home along the back of her neck and around her shoulder blades. She hums in contentment when I am finished and turns to face me.

"Thank you." Never have we physically stood so close to one another, and it is a dangerous game when neither of us has any clothing on. The physical touching triggers the mate bond to stir to life.

"You are welcome." I clear my throat, so glad that she cannot see my hard erection beneath the water. "We should go now. You need to eat."

She rolls her eyes at me. "I just ate before we came. I want to stay until I'm a prune."

I splash the look off her face. "Fine."

She gasps and splashes me back, until we're fighting and laughing and water is going everywhere. I grab her, pinning her against my body by wrapping my arms around her so she can't splash me anymore. Her laugh trails off, and, looking into each other's eyes, we realize our naked bodies are pressed against each other, my throbbing cock wedged between us, with one of my hands holding her firmly on her behind. She tries to wiggle free, and I close my eyes, nostrils flaring as she rubs herself against my cock. Instantly, I let her go, stepping back slightly so we are no longer touching. I grip the base of my cock tightly, aching to spill my seed everywhere, to cover her in it, to fill her with it until it drips from her cunt. I turn away from her, running my hand over my head. I hear water dripping onto the rocky floor as she gets out of the spring. I keep my back turned to give her time to dry herself and cover up.

"Asterion?"

I turn in the water to face her. She's wrapped up in the fabric I use for my loincloth. It's twirled around her so she looks like a little silkworm, her violet hair slick over her shoulders, turning the fabric semi-transparent. In her hands, she holds a crumpled-up dark lump of something. She spreads it out, the fabric stiff, and I suddenly know what it is she is holding.

"You should put that down." I scratch the back of my neck as shame floods me.

"This is my jacket." She turns it over. "What is this?" She picks at the off-white stains spread over and dried into the fabric. She brings it to her nose to sniff.

"No, do not!" I yell, climbing out of the water to take it from her.

She looks at me as if I have grown two heads, then seems to suddenly realize why I am so horrified.

"Asterion! Did you come on my jacket?"

23

KATIE

Anger douses any arousal that was simmering beneath the surface after being pressed against his body, his giant cock flush against my stomach. Now, seeing it front on for the first time, that thing *could* be used as a weapon.

I drop my cum-stained jacket and spin on my heel, careful not to slip, and storm out of the bathing cave and back toward Asterion's hut. I can't believe he used my jacket as some sort of cum rag! I can hear Asterion scrambling in the cave to chase after me, scooping me up as I head back toward his hut.

"Put me down, you—you beast!" I screech, hammering my fists on his slick back, and get an eyeful of a very tight ass as we make it back inside. He sets me back on the floor, along with the sack of things he took with us and our now clean, wet clothes.

I stand in the middle of Asterion's home in nothing but this wrap of fabric, and I'm finding it hard to maintain my dignity without any fucking clothes on.

I haven't needed my knife, nor have I had any pockets to keep it in, so I've kept it tucked away between the furs. Close enough for me to reach it at night, when I might need it the most. I search for it now, flinging a fur to the side.

"What are you looking for?"

I shoot a glare at him, throwing a fur back down, and turn to him.

"Where is my knife?"

He pushes off from the counter, his cock erect and weeping from the tip, and steps toward me. He likes this game of cat and mouse, and I try desperately not to look.

"This knife?" With a flick of his hand, the blade is between his fingers, the handle pointed in my direction. "It really is not safe to sleep with a blade."

I growl, attempting to snatch it back from him, but he only lifts it out of my reach.

"Give it to me." *So I can stab you with it*, I almost say.

He leans into my face. "How bad do you want it, little viper?"

Arousal angrily flares to life, ignited by his sultry gravel tone. I begin to feel wet despite being pissed at him for violating my jacket.

He steps into my space, causing me to back up or be nose to nose with him.

The backs of my legs hit the raised platform where the furs make up his bed. I squeak as I tip backwards into the little nest I've made. He climbs in after me, his dick bobbing, and I shuffle backwards until I can't go any further.

He cages me in with his arms. My heart beats rapidly in my chest like a rat caught in a snake's nest. Predator and prey, and I don't think I'm the viper in this situation. Having his body this close to mine sends my hormones into a frenzy, already wound tight from our closeness in the hot spring. The mate bond has it so I can't tell if I want to fight him or fuck him.

"How bad do you want it, little viper?" he repeats, rubbing his snout in the crook of my neck, inhaling deeply.

I want it so bad.

The knife, I mean.

"If you can take it, you can have it back," he whispers in my ear, bringing the handle of the knife to my skin, tracing it down the side of my neck and over the fabric wrapped around me. Goose pimples erupt along my skin from his touch.

His pupils are blown, and I know the mate bond is driving him just as mad. Each day, it gets worse. I feel like I am feverish and wet all the time, and all the little innuendos and the dirty way he says such innocent things have me wanting to hold onto his horns while I ride his face.

He reaches the bottom of the fabric and looks down at me, and then to where he holds the blade, the handle of the knife teasing along my thigh in place of his fingers. I suck my bottom lip between my teeth, at war with myself. I so desperately want his touch just a little higher, but I'm also not sure this is something we should be doing.

Fuck it.

If life has taught me anything, it's that we only get to live it once. I've got my second chance at freedom, so why should I hold myself back anymore? The thought is as exhilarating as it is freeing.

My lips part with soft pants in anticipation, and my legs fall open. Maintaining eye contact, he leans into me, pressing his nose into the fabric over my groin, and inhales. My hips buck slightly, rubbing myself against his muzzle, eager for more. More pressure, more anything. He grins as he pulls back, and my tongue darts out to wet my lips. He copies me, pressing his tongue into the fabric, soaking it with his saliva until there's a wet patch where my pussy is. Teasing me by not even touching me.

He takes the handle of my pocketknife and traces it over the wet patch. I whimper as he presses it between my legs and against my sensitive clit.

"Do you still want your knife, little viper?"

A thin sheen of sweat has broken out across my forehead, my bottom lip between my teeth as I nod.

"Are you going to take it from me?" He quirks his head with a smirk.

This fucking—

I roll us, which is no small feat, until I am sitting astride him, my legs spread wide across his broad body, his hard dick flush against his stomach, weeping pre-cum into his fur. From this angle, I can see rungs of gold metal lining the underside of his cock, and my mouth pops open. The column of his dick is pierced. That is a problem for another day, because right now is just for me.

He's still holding the blade of the knife, the sharp edge awfully close to his dick. The handle is now wedged between us, right against my sensitive nub. I give an involuntary buck against it, seeking the friction I crave. It feels so wrong to use it like this, but I also can't find it in me to care. All I care about right now is coming.

I grind against it again, the blade biting into the skin of his hand, a thin line of red welting. The fabric rides up my hips, exposing the dark curls between my legs, and he groans as he watches me move.

"Do you want me to stop?" I ask between pants as I roll my hips.

"Do not dare stop. I want you to use me, little viper. I want you to come all over me."

I can feel my wetness coating the insides of my thighs as I grind against the handle of the knife, but it's not enough.

"I need more," I whine.

"Fates," he curses, shifting me so that his cock is between my folds instead, the balls of his piercings rolling against my skin as I grind against him, coating him in my wetness.

"Mm, better." I sigh, setting the pace, working myself against his cock.

"Lean forward," he grunts, and I cock an eyebrow at him. "Do you trust me?"

Not that long ago, I would've said no. But now it's different. He has made it impossible for me not to trust him. I nod, leaning forward and resting my head on his chest. I feel something firm press at my entrance and realize what he's doing. He rolls his hips beneath me, sliding his cock between my folds, able to hit my clit better at this angle with his piercings. The handle of the knife edges inside me with each thrust, working in place of a finger.

My breathing wobbles as he slides between my thighs and works the handle in and out of me, covering it in my juices.

"What was your plan for this knife, little viper?" he growls, the vibration adding to the abundance of sensations. "Were you going to stab me with it? Again?"

I lift my head, nodding as I moan while he works me faster.

"Even after I saved your life?"

I moan my release, my walls pulsing around the handle of the pocketknife as I come undone.

Asterion gently eases it out of me before licking it clean and flipping me onto my back. He buries his nose at my core and licks every inch of me clean until I'm gasping.

He smirks, snicking the blade shut and dropping the small knife at my side in the furs.

"Since you took it so well."

24

ASTERION

I ignore the throbbing of my hard cock as I admire my mate, sated with heavy-lidded eyes in my furs. I get myself dressed, tying a loincloth around my waist. As much as I want to know what it is like to bury myself deep inside her, her body is not yet ready. I prepare a meal for us to replenish her energy, and she slips out of the furs to join me in the cooking area she has dubbed a 'kitchen,' humming along to a song as we work in sync.

She has not bothered to get dressed, still wrapped up in the fabric I gave her. Her hair is mussed, and she has a healthy pink flush on her cheeks. I cannot help myself. Now that we have been intimate in some way, I want to always touch her. I pull her into me, and she squeals as I sandwich her between me and the mud-brick counter.

I nuzzle her neck with a groan. "You smell so good."

She huffs. "You're always saying I smell!"

"Little viper." I trail kisses down the side of her neck. "It was never about you smelling bad." I kiss along her collarbone. "It was that you smelled so good, it drove me mad with desire." I press my still very erect cock against her stomach for her to feel my arousal.

Her mouth pops open. "I thought it was because I smelled horrible!" She smacks at my chest, and I chuckle. I turn her so that her back is to me, and together, we cut the rest of the vegetables, using her hands as my hands. She presses her backside further into me and does a little wiggle every now and then, keeping my cock aching for her.

"If you do not stop pressing yourself into me, I will have to bend you over this counter and bring you to climax again."

"I have no idea what you're talking about." She flicks a smirk over her shoulder at me, purposely rolling her hips once more.

I growl in her ear. "Was before not enough for my eager little mate?"

My fingers tug at the little tie at the top of the fabric above her breasts, letting it come undone so that I can unravel her. I have yet to see her completely bare, and my mouth salivates at having the chance to do so right now.

"How about we play a little game?" The fabric falls to the ground, leaving her bare back exposed to me, and two perfect little globes of milky flesh.

She turns. "What kind of game?"

I am momentarily speechless, dazed by breasts peaked with soft pink nipples. My gaze trails down to the patch of dark curls between her legs that I caught a glimpse of earlier.

I lift her onto the counter, moving everything out of the way, and position myself between her legs. "The game is to see if I can wring an orgasm out of you for every time you ran from me."

"Seems like an unfair game if I get all the prizes." Her eyes twinkle with mischief.

"I need no prizes." I drop to my knees before her and throw her legs over my shoulders, dragging her as close to the edge as possible. She leans back, propping herself up with her elbows to give me better access. The perfect mate. "I already have you."

I nuzzle into her core, swiping at her folds with my tongue until she cries out. She grabs one of my horns, and I chuckle as she grinds herself against my mouth.

"Oh fuck." She moans.

I lick and suck until she is a dripping, writhing mess all over my counter, and then I slide one finger inside her, stretching her tight, wet hole. She pants, and I swirl my tongue around her clit to get her to relax around it before I curl the tip of my finger to find that sweet spot inside her. I rub that spot and suck at her clit until she clenches around me with a moan, her thighs snapping shut around my head as she holds my mouth exactly where she wants it by my horn until she has finished coming.

"That one was for running from me in the labyrinth."

She pants, her chest rising and falling rapidly as I stand, pressing myself between her thighs, and licking up the column of her neck. I hook one leg over my arm while my fingers find her center once more. I ease one back inside her, gently thrusting it in and out while leaning down to swirl my tongue over her nipple. She bucks against me as my thumb glides over her sensitive nub in just a tease. I move my mouth to her other nipple, sucking and catching it between my teeth ever so gently. Still, I work my finger inside her until she's slick once more. I switch fingers, lubricating a second with a few thrusts before joining them together. Slowly easing two digits inside her, I hike her leg higher over the crook of my elbow until she's falling back to lie across the counter, completely giving herself over to my ministrations. The second orgasm hits her out of nowhere with a silent scream, her back arching up from the counter, and her hand gripping my forearm. My home smells like strawberries, sweet and syrupy.

"That was for cutting the rope the second night." I lean down and kiss her navel.

She whimpers as I gently pick her up in my arms and carry her to the furs, her body completely spent.

"Do you want me to—?" She looks at my cock standing to attention and weeping from the lack of it. I appreciate the offer, and I ache to take her up on it, but not yet.

"I do not wish for you to exert yourself." I grab a wet cloth and clean her up before tucking her in, and then go back to making her something to eat while she rests. She will need all her energy to keep up with me, and I plan to see that she is properly cared for.

Now that I know she was not part of a horrible trick and that she has no desire to go home, the built-up resentment and anger I harbored—not toward her, but *because* of her—has faded away to dust. Katie is sharp and feisty, traits I admire in a mate, and beneath that tough-girl exterior, she yearns to be taken care of. Just as I wish to be the one to do it. I would find satisfaction in each day I am able to fill her with food, and eventually my cock, and perhaps one day, a babe.

First, I must make sure she is in full health. Her recovery has been a slow one, her head wound a more delicate injury than most. Perhaps it would not be so had she been in peak physical condition prior, but her body was already suffering. I make a note to visit the spring every day now that she can make the short trip. Nonetheless, I believe it will be good for her to be waited on hand and foot, to be shown how a mate should be treated. She should want for nothing and have all her needs met, and I am a more than willing participant.

The mate bond thrums beneath my skin like a secondary pulse, sated because our mate is sated, for now. How long until it drives us completely mad, and will I be able to deny it what it wants? I loathe to hurt the little viper, and there is part of me that knows that right now, she will not be able to take me without injury.

25

KATIE

I settle into this peaceful life, and my mind is calmer for it. I swap the comfort of sleeping with my knife for Asterion in the furs, no longer confined to the chair he slept on while I was healing.

I rest a lot, and eat a lot, and though I don't have access to a mirror, I can feel the way my body has changed in the way my clothing fits. Bony hips and protruding ribs have filled out into a softness I haven't seen in a long time. I almost weep with joy at clawing another piece of me back.

I ask Asterion to teach me to garden, and I've never seen his face light up as much as when he's explaining the difference between potatoes and yams.

I gradually begin to have fewer nightmares. Greg's face no longer haunts me in my sleep, nor the horrible cackle of an old lady as I'm smothered in darkness. Screams of terror are replaced with screams of pleasure when waking to Asterion's head between my legs, or his warm mouth on my breast while his fingers bring me to climax.

I long to give him the pleasure he seeks too. I imagine what it would be like to take his cock in my mouth and roll his piercings along my tongue. But he doesn't let me, adamant that I'm not recovered enough yet. Instead, he distracts me by wringing another orgasm from me until I can barely keep my eyes open.

I climb out of the giant nest of furs and stand in the doorway, looking for Asterion. I expect to see him in his vegetable garden, but he's not there. I make my way around the back of the hut to use the makeshift toilet, only to find it already occupied. Asterion stands there with his cock in hand.

"Oh, sorry!" I yelp, turning my back to him. Oh my god, where else would he be if not in the garden? I smack my forehead.

The groan he makes is a familiar sound. Heat rushes to my face as I realize he's not using the toilet for its usual purposes. I can't help but peek over my shoulder at him. He must not have heard me, or if he did, he shows no sign of caring. His fist strokes and twists around his gigantic dick. His head is tilted back as he holds something over his snout. Is that—

"Is that my shirt?!" I turn fully to face him, my hands on my hips.

He grunts, his seed spurting into the hole in the ground as he grips the base of his cock that expands beneath his fist. His breath quivers as he wrings the last few drops from himself. My eyes widen. I have *never* seen a dick do that before.

"All yours, little viper." He hums while walking toward me, pulling my shirt on over my head, and slapping me on the ass as he leaves me to my business.

I'm lost for words, looking back at him over my shoulder, a little hurt. He has not allowed me to touch him in that way at all, despite how many times I've tried. I don't know if I've done something wrong or if it's something he doesn't like. Nasty thoughts rear up in my head—Greg telling me how useless I am, and that I'm no good at anything. I know they're not true. But the rejection stings just the same, stirring up these feelings of never being enough.

I trudge back into the hut where Asterion is making me breakfast. He puts a plate of it down on the table before cocking his head at me and sniffing.

"What is wrong?"

"I'm fine."

He grabs my chin to tilt my face to him. "Your scent has soured. Do not lie to me."

Ugh, the cursed smell, always giving me away. Mostly, when I'm horny, though, so it's not usually a problem. But I've since learned it smells rotten when I'm hurt or angry or sad, also giving away my feelings to Asterion.

"I could do that for you, you know."

"I do not want—"

"Me to exert myself. I know." I roll my eyes.

He scowls. "I did not realize I had become so repetitive."

"I just—it's something I want to do for you. And for me. It hurts when you push me away." I struggle with the words to describe how I feel. Sharing is something I'm still getting used to after Greg.

He sits back in his chair, contemplating. "Okay."

I look up, eyes wide. "Really?"

"Only if you can walk to the bathing spring and back again without needing to rest."

I scowl. That's a dirty move. He knows I've only just been able to make that trip without needing to be carried some of the way. But I'm determined.

I jut my chin out. "Fine."

"Fine." He smirks. "Now eat your breakfast before it goes cold."

I never thought I'd be negotiating hand jobs over breakfast, but here I am.

Once we're done eating, we leave for the spring. The idea of having Asterion at my mercy has made me determined to make it there and back without any help.

I flash him a coy smile, and then I turn and skip the rest of the way, squealing with laughter as Asterion comes up behind me and scoops me up into his arms.

"This doesn't count!" I cackle as we plunge into the warm water together.

He lathers me up with soap, and I don't bother to argue. He has taken the role of cleaning me upon himself, and honestly, who am I to say no when it comes to a head massage and someone else to comb out my tangles?

Asterion is extra thorough when it comes to lathering up my breasts. Heat floods my core before I find his fingers there as well, slipping inside me briefly enough to leave me wanting more before resuming his cleaning on other parts of my body.

A plan comes to mind, and I think this might be an opportunity for me to provide him with some relief as well. I take the soap berries from him and lather up my own hands, taking them and running them down his chest. His hands falter, eyes closing, and a stuttered breath shows me exactly how tense he is. He's been so patient; it's only fair that I get to show him my gratitude for everything he's done for me. I massage the muscles I can reach, trailing my hands up and down his arms, circling his back, and then running them down his abs until my slicked hands reach down to his already erect cock.

He sucks in a breath as I take his hard cock in both hands, sliding up and down, and running my fingers over his piercings. He frowns, and I know he's moments from pulling away from me, so I must make it so he can't help himself. I squeeze, tightening my grip, and his hips jerk. His jaw goes slack as I grip him tight and move my hands, twisting at the base like I saw him do to himself. He lets out a guttural groan, and I know I've won this round.

"That is a dirty trick, little viper." He pants.

"I just want to show you how thankful I am." I smirk slyly, pumping him beneath the water until we're making little ripples in the spring.

He grunts, picking me up and placing me on the stony floor at the edge of the spring before pressing himself against me, his cock and his piercings flush against my pussy. He grabs the back of my neck, pulling me into a fierce kiss while rubbing himself against my sensitive flesh. He gently pushes me down until I'm lying on the warm, slick stone and then soaps me up once more, covering my thighs in a foamy lather before clamping them shut around his cock, wedging it between my folds, and begins to thrust.

His piercings roll against my clit, causing me to buck against him, and he pins me down with a hand on my chest, my legs held flush against his body with the other arm while he fucks my thighs.

We moan in tandem. Asterion loses all semblance of control as his pace picks up, using my body to get himself off, and I love every moment of it. He lets out a choked gasp as he comes, rivulets spurting from between my thighs to coat my stomach. He growls, his hips stuttering as the base of his cock expands. His hand moves down from my chest to rub his spilled seed into my skin. His pupils are blown as he swipes his fingers through the creamy spend, then pushes it inside my wet, needy pussy.

"Mine," he growls, and I gasp as he removes his finger and rubs it across my bottom lip, my tongue darting out on instinct to wipe it away. We taste sweet together, and tart, like strawberries.

He continues to fuck me with his finger, stretching me out, and hitting that sweet spot that makes my toes curl. He uses some of his cum to help lubricate, adding a second finger and pumping inside me until my pussy is so wet and slick, the squelching noises that come from me should be illegal. I writhe beneath him, grinding into the palm of his hand until my climax crests, clenching down on his fingers and pulsing around him as I come.

He slows, waiting for me to relax again before resuming his ministrations, adding a third finger into the mix. I feel the burn as I stretch around him. He takes more of his cum from my stomach and swirls it around my clit before rubbing it around my entrance and using it to aid his fingers in stretching me out. I pant, breathless and dazed from pleasure. Somehow, my plan has been turned around on me. I'm not mad about it.

Suddenly, his fingers are gone, and I feel so empty before he lines up the tip of his cock with my entrance. YES! I could combust with how ready I am for him to finally fill me up. The tip pushes past my entrance, and then all of a sudden, it's like Asterion comes to his senses, pulling out of me with a hiss. NO!

He looks distraught, and I lean up on my elbows.

"I—apologize." The words stick in his throat, and he clears it with a cough.

"There is no excuse." He says it so sincerely, I could weep. "I promise it will not happen again, even if I must wound myself in order to stop."

"Alright, Romeo. No need for the self-flagellation." I sit up with a huff, grabbing his face between my hands. "I want this. I want you." I look him square in the eyes, desperate for him to see the truth in my words. How can I get him to see that I'm okay?

"You are not ready. I do not want to injure you. I lost control." He hangs his head in shame.

I tilt his chin up, so he has to look at me. "It is not for you to say whether I am ready or not. Have you not thought that perhaps I want you to lose control?"

Confusion passes through his gaze before widening in clarity.

I slowly get to my feet, legs shaky beneath me, and for the first time, I choose to run.

26

ASTERION

MINE.

I leap out of the water after my mate. Her tinkling laughter echoes through the labyrinth, and I bellow from the thrill of the beginning of a hunt. I follow the thick scent of strawberries, my feet slapping the hard ground, stones rattling along the path. My mate is wet and aroused; I can scent her dripping for me. I must show everyone she is my mate; find her and fuck her and fill her with my seed.

My mate. Mine.

27

KATIE

I am free.

Hair whips around my face as I run stark naked through dark tunnels. I don't know where I'm heading, instantly lost. But I know Asterion will find me. I'm betting on it. The idea of him chasing me down in the dark gets my blood pumping inside my veins, the adrenaline making me even wetter than he's already managed. I know he won't hurt me; he's proven as much in the tender way he cares for me every day.

My bare feet pound against the stone almost in time with my racing heart. After months of being on the run, fear following me around every corner, it is both exhilarating and cathartic choosing to run for myself. Knowing that when I am caught, I will be punished, not with pain, but with pleasure.

Asterion's feet ring out behind me, quickly tracking me down and catching up. A nervous giggle escapes me at knowing he is so close, instantly giving myself away. He rounds the corner in a matter of footsteps, steam billowing from his nostrils, before lifting me off my feet. My scream turns into a laugh as I lean in and place a kiss on his cheek.

"My mate." He grunts.

"Yours." I caress his cheek before he drops to his knees, flipping me onto my stomach.

The ground is warm beneath my cheek and rough against my nipples as he grabs me by the hips and lifts me, so my ass is up in the air, before swiping straight to my core with a lick of his tongue. I moan loudly, unabashedly, in the dark while he drives his wet tongue inside me until I'm wriggling in his grasp for more.

SLAP.

His hand comes down on my ass cheek, and I let out a yelp from surprise more than pain, until his fingers spear me, relentlessly thrusting, turning the sting into pleasure and my yelp into a moan. Now I see the appeal of a spanking, my skin tingling with anticipation. I'm so wet I can feel it on the inside of my thighs as

Asterion works a third finger inside me once more. There's no burn this time, arousal aiding the stretch until he adds a fourth finger, and I don't know how I could possibly fit any more. I'm surprised at the tenderness as he works his fingers inside me until I'm shaking, and then there's a wetness at my asshole, his tongue rimming the puckered hole. I can barely breathe from the sensory overwhelm, and my orgasm rocks me hard and fast. I scream as my walls clench around his fingers, and then they're gone. I look over my shoulder as he licks them clean, and with no time for recovery, he lines his cock up with my entrance.

I could weep when he pushes past the outer ring, filling me up with his warm, silky cock, his piercings massaging my walls as he edges himself in inch by inch. I'm so full, it takes my breath away.

"I don't think it's going to fit." He grunts, clearly not completely out of his mind with lust.

Oh, hell no. "It'll fit."

Before he can withdraw, I push myself backwards onto him, until I'm practically sitting in his lap, his cock fully seated inside me. I feel so ridiculously full that I need a moment to relax around him and adjust, but I have a deep sense of satisfaction when I take all of it. He grunts in surprise, and I begin to move, testing out the limitations, slowly sliding myself up and down, groaning as his piercings rub against my G-spot. His hands band around my hips, taking over for me when I find a good rhythm until he's fucking me from below.

"Oh fuck," I cry with pleasure.

He finally does what I've been wanting from him and loses control, slamming into me. I band an arm around the back of his neck to brace myself, while his other hand finds my clit, swirling over it with the perfect amount of pressure.

"My. Mate." He grunts in time with his thrusts. "Mine. Mine. Mine."

I can't say anything. I'm pretty sure his dick is in my throat at this point.

"I am going to fuck you and fill you up with my seed." Thrust.

"I want you so full it spills out of you, running down your thighs." Thrust.

"I want everyone to smell me on you and know exactly who you belong to." Thrust.

"Who do you belong to?" Thrust.

"Whose mate are you?" Thrust.

"Yours!" I cry, my orgasm crashing through me at full throttle, pulsing around his length.

"Fates, your cunt grips me so tight." He slams into me one more time and comes with a roar. I can feel the warmth of his cum fill me as his hips stutter, and then there's suddenly a lot of pressure at my entrance.

"My knot," Asterion grunts out, attempting to remove himself.

"No!" I yell, locking myself onto him. "I want it. I want everything."

He kisses along my shoulder as our breathing evens out. He lies us down on our sides, his arms banded around me so we can cuddle while we wait for his knot to soften.

"Are you okay?" he asks, kissing my hair.

"Peachy," I reply sleepily.

We lay there in a random dark tunnel of the labyrinth, our bodies linked, our fingers threaded with one another's, and I've never felt more at peace than in this moment.

"Why do you think the Fates brought me here?" I whisper into the dark once we catch our breath.

Asterion hums. "I do not think the Fates have any reason for the things they do besides sowing chaos upon the world. They should not have been able to bring you here at all, and I have been wondering if they have set something in motion that cannot be undone. It should not have snowed that night you fell, and I can only assume the barrier that protects us is malfunctioning."

"What does that mean, if the barrier comes down?"

"We will be exposed to the outside world once again. Tell me, do you think your world would welcome us?"

Dread fills my stomach, and I shake my head. No, the world is not ready to be face to face with mythical creatures.

"I may not know why the Fates have brought you here, but I cannot be mad for it. Living a solitary life, frozen in time, I never thought I would get a chance at having a mate. I know you do not wish to return to your home, but I hope that you will find one here with me that makes you happy."

I cozy into him, feeling the beginnings of his knot soften and his cum leak from me as he pulls out. It's like he can't help himself as his fingers collect it and push it back inside me. I pull his face down to mine and kiss him. "I am home."

The End.

186

GLOSSARY

Asterion – Ahs-steer-ee-on

Katie – Kay-tee

Aeolia – Ee-ol-ee-ah

Pierian – Pie-ree-an

Drakon – Drack-un

Ladon – Lay-dun

Pytho – Pie-thoe

Moirai – Moy-rye

Lachesis – Lack-uh-siss

Acknowledgements

This book was so fun to write. As soon as I sat down the words just flowed out of me. I even made it on deadline!

I really want to thank my husband for being my biggest hype man. For all the things he does around the house and for helping with all the businesses he didn't sign up for. None of this would be possible without him holding down the fort while I hunker down and write for hours on end.

Special mention to Nikki who fuelled me with snacks and concert ticket bribes, and who was also one of my alpha and beta readers. Your attention to detail makes a difference.

My alpha and betas! I had more eyes on this manuscript than any before it. Thank you to alphas: Navarda, Bree, and Jennifer. Thank you to betas: Heidi and Tamika.

As always, to my fab editor Laura, thanks for holding me accountable.

I hope you all enjoy Mated Minotaur and I'll see you in the next one.

ABOUT THE AUTHOR

Lex Logan is a queer and neurodivergent author living in Australia
with her husband and two children.

When she's not cooking up more stories than she can physically
write, she's running her indie romance bookstore – Tales & Tomes,
or rotting in bed with a book.

Visit her website: www.lexloganauthor.com

ALSO BY LEX LOGAN

<u>Mated Myths</u>

Seducing Scylla

Tempting Triton

Mated Minotaur